The
Overnight
Fame of
Steffi
McBride

The Overnight Fame of Steffi McBride

AJ Crofts

JOHN BLAKE

Published by John Blake Publishing Ltd,
3 Bramber Court, 2 Bramber Road,
London W14 9PB, England

www.blake.co.uk

First published in paperback in 2008

ISBN: 978-1-84454-652-7

British Library Cataloguing-in-Publication Data:

A catalogue record for this book is available from the British Library.

Design by www.envydesign.co.uk

Printed in Great Britain by Creative Print and Design, Blaina, Wales

1 3 5 7 9 10 8 6 4 2

Papers used by John Blake Publishing are natural, recyclable products made from
wood grown in sustainable forests. The manufacturing processes conform to the
environmental regulations of the country of origin.

Praise for *The Overnight Fame of Steffi McBride*

'I've never read a novel about a rising star that portrays so vividly and accurately the processes and their impact on the character's life, their world and their relationships. The book brilliantly gets inside the mind of a young woman on her way up, battling against the odds, her loves and the prices she has to pay. I was hooked from the first page to the last and read it through almost non-stop.'

Peter James, film producer and best-selling author of *Dead Simple*.

www.peterjames.com

'Seeing such a self-composed and attractive woman talking about her big break, I found it hard not to draw parallels with the unfolding tragedy of Britney Spears'

Linda Jones www.trashionista.com

To Susan, Alex, Amy, Olivia and Jess,
with all my love

www.steffimcbride.com

Chapter One

No one told us who they were. There was no way of knowing, they didn't look like anything special, just sitting in the corner of the room, staring at us. The bloke was jotting down notes on a pad like he was a journalist or something, but so what? I'd have expected them to have a bit more about them considering who they turned out to be.

The man had a streaming cold, which had made his nose go bright red from wiping. I remember thinking I didn't want to go anywhere near him in case I caught it. He had a big old jumper on with a high rolled-up collar, the sort of thing our dad might wear when he went fishing, and not too clean either.

The woman was old, well over fifty I'd say, with about two inches of grey-brown roots showing in her red hair. It was funny that she hadn't bothered to do anything about them because it looked like quite an expensive cut, pretty trendy for someone her age. She was wearing dark glasses, even though it was evening and the lights in the hall weren't that bright, so I assumed she had a cold as well. She certainly looked pasty enough to be ill.

There was no reason for us to think anything of them;

Dora often had friends sitting in on the classes, or people who came and went. Sometimes they were old actors and actresses none of us recognised, who would chip in with a bit of advice themselves once things warmed up, but more often they never said a word and Dora never introduced them.

If I'd known who they were I might have taken the time to put on a bit of make-up, and I don't know that I would have let myself go emotionally in quite the same way I did, so it was probably for the best that Dora didn't announce their presence there. Actually, she probably did it on purpose, because she's a wily old bird is Dora.

I look pretty crap without make-up – and that isn't me being modest, it's a fact. I'm about the only person on our estate from a mixed family who has come out looking like a fucking albino. All the others come out looking gorgeous with perfect, caramel complexions and I came out even paler than Dad. When we're out as a family, I must look like the freak puppy of the litter. Still, could have been worse: I could have been completely ginger and freckled, like Dad and all his McBride relations in Ireland. I've seen photos of them and it's a shocking sight. I've never met any of them in person, so I dare say they make up for it with wit and charm!

If I don't wear make-up my face disappears. When people first see me with make-up they're amazed by the transformation, which is pretty insulting really. Dora says it's great for an actress because I'm a 'blank canvas', and I know what she means: I can paint almost anything on my face, make myself into anything I want, whereas the ones who actually have some colour have to get rid of it all first and start again.

It would still be nice to at least have some dark eyelashes so it doesn't look as if I have no eyes at all.

Don't get me wrong. I do usually make an effort and paint myself up before I go out – before I even go down to breakfast, most days – but sometimes I just can't be arsed, and this was one of those times.

I wasn't feeling that well, to be honest, which might have been another reason why I got a bit emotional. It was really tiring to work all day and then go out and have Dora screaming abuse at you all evening, and sometimes it got a bit much, especially with everything that had gone on at home the previous evening. There wasn't much point in making an effort to paint myself up just to have it all steamed off again by the dishwashers in the hotel kitchens where I'd been working all day, and I'd had to rush straight to Dora's from there and I hadn't had time to have anything to eat and my period had just started and ... well, that's probably as much detail as you want.

Because I was a few minutes late I hadn't had much time to think about what I was going to do for my piece and Dora was being a bit arsey about me 'holding up the class', so I just launched myself into it and once I started talking things sort of spiralled out of control.

'Just tell us something from your life that makes you feel really sad,' Dora had said. 'Steffi, you go first and make it truthful, for God's sake.'

That was completely out of order because I was always truthful when it came to acting and stuff. In fact, I think I'm always pretty truthful about everything, which gets me into

3

more than a little trouble. There was no time to think up anything clever to do, and the fight from the previous night was still fresh in my mind, so I went for it.

'I love my dad to bits,' I said, pulling as much air into my lungs as I could, knowing I was going to need it if I was going to get through this in one piece, 'but sometimes he can be a real bastard.' I noticed the two visitors watching me intently but I didn't care. I quite liked shocking people. Dora wanted something truthful and I always wanted to do what she asked. She was an old bag but I liked her and I respected her, even if her career had gone down the toilet and she had ended up teaching a bunch of no-hoper kids who all wanted to be stars.

'It's the fucking Guinness,' I said, 'especially when he mixes it with vodka. He's Irish and a ginger and he has a fucking terrible temper. Last night he'd already been to the pub before he got home, and I guess we were all making a lot of noise and the house was a mess, but usually he doesn't care about that sort of thing. We all know when he's going to pick a fight and we try to stay out of his way, but for some reason we didn't spot the signs last night, even Mum didn't. She's usually good at that, being a social worker and dealing with shitheads all day long, but she was distracted with getting us all our tea and stuff and she just didn't pay him as much attention as she should have and he went off like a fucking atomic bomb. He had her by the throat, and his hands are as big as shovels and they were choking the life out of her. We were all screaming at him to put her down but none of us was strong enough to pull him off. Her eyes were bulging like they were going to pop out and she was jerking around

4

like she was in her death throes. He'd actually lifted her off her feet, pinned her to the wall.'

As I told the story, I could picture the scene completely. I forgot I was talking to an audience – well, a sort of audience – I just wanted to describe truthfully how it had felt for those few moments when I thought Dad was killing Mum. I knew I was crying, but I didn't bother to wipe the tears. (Maybe a little bit of my brain was staying objective and telling me that a few tears would add to the dramatic impact.) I could even feel some snot sliding out of my nose.

I didn't look around at the audience until I'd said all I wanted to say and only then did I realise the hall had gone completely silent. They were all crying, or staring at me with shocked faces and their hands covering their mouths. Even the two strangers were searching for tissues and blowing their noses, but that might have been because of their colds.

I felt a bit embarrassed to have made such an exhibition of myself, but proud too because I knew I'd done what Dora had asked of me. I had been truthful and it had had a dramatic effect on everyone listening. I felt a little bit guilty too, squealing on Dad about something that should have been private family business really, but serve him right. If he was going to behave like an animal then he had to take the consequences. Nobody else in the class came from our estate, so I was pretty sure word wouldn't get back that I was being indiscreet about private family business.

'Thank you, Steffi,' Dora said, as if I'd just read a particularly nice poem to the class. 'Who would like to go next?'

I took my place among the others and it wasn't long before

I'd stopped shaking and was listening to them. Most of them were pretty crap, if I'm going to be honest. One of them talked about the day his cat was run over, another one talked about when her parents told her they were going to get divorced, but none of them made me remotely want to cry.

I don't want to sound like I'm up myself or anything, but most of them are truly crap actors. Dora's place is not the Royal Academy of Dramatic Art. I know that for a fact because I went there, and to about six other posh drama schools. We had this teacher at school, Dave, who used to teach English and direct the school plays and all that. I really liked him, and not just because he thought I was good. He just had something about him that most of the other teachers didn't have, like a passion for his subject. I guess he had fucked up as much as Dora to end up teaching in a school as crap as ours, but he didn't seem to care, he still seemed to love what he was doing.

He introduced us to Shakespeare, which most of the others thought was bollocks, but I really loved it. Even though it had all those weird old-fashioned words and everything, it seemed to have a rhythm, which made it understandable to me, a bit like good rap music. I just liked saying it out loud. Dave put on *Romeo and Juliet* for the parents on Founders Day and, even though I had to kiss Creepy Malone, who was playing Romeo, I got a real buzz from it. (Creepy really seemed to enjoy the kissing, but I was mainly concentrating on avoiding his zits and his tongue.)

Dave said I was good enough to act professionally, but when I mentioned it at home the consensus was that it was

6

a come-on line and Dave was just trying to get into my knickers. Actually, I wouldn't have minded too much if he had, but he didn't even try, which is a bit insulting now I think about it. He was one of those teachers you just know you can trust to behave honourably, which is kind of strangely attractive.

Because they had all been so fucking negative about it at home I didn't let on that I was going to audition at the drama schools, so I had to pay for it myself and it cost me a fucking fortune. They charge, like, thirty quid each just to listen to you and then tell you to fuck off home. Anyway, I did it and it was a real buzz, but there weren't many people like me at the auditions. They weren't exactly posh, well only some of them, but they mostly weren't estate people. Maybe some of the northerners were; it's hard to tell with their accents. I loved listening to all the different voices. In fact, I pretty much loved everything about those audition days. Only one of them actually offered me a place, but Dave said that was brilliant – he said that most people have to go back year after year and still never get in. He also said it was unusual for them to take someone so young. He was so impressed, and so sweet, I just wanted to suck his face off.

For a few days I was walking on air. It actually looked like I might make it, but when I sat down with Mum and Dad and really thought it through I could see we couldn't afford it. Mum kept saying we would find a way, and that there were grants and all the rest, but Dad went ballistic, shouting and yelling, wanting to know who I thought I was that I deserved to have three years' playing around at their expense. I was

7

quite surprised how adamant he was, like I'd suggested going on the game or something.

I suppose I could see where he was coming from. Maybe if I had been going to university, like Mum did, so that I could hold a proper job at the end – but just so that I could be an actress, when most of the time they're all out of work, did seem a bit of a liberty. With six of us, too, they would have to treat us all the same and they were working all the hours God sent already, so in the end I decided I just couldn't do it to them. Mind you, money wouldn't have been so tight if Dad didn't stop off at the pub on the way home every night, and puff his way through a couple of packs of cigarettes a day. None of us has ever had the nerve to point that particular fact out to him, though, even though we all think it.

I think Dave was even more disappointed than I was. He offered to come round and talk to Mum and Dad and I had to explain that it wasn't exactly them, that it was more my own conscience stopping me. I didn't tell him that if he came round trying to tell Dad how to bring up his children he was likely to end up having his face kicked in. He just kept shaking his head and saying it was a great waste and that I shouldn't throw away my whole life just because it would be hard and I would have to expect to make some sacrifices at the beginning if I wanted to achieve anything worthwhile. That really pissed me off and I started shouting at him, telling him he didn't understand the first thing about our family and how much Mum and Dad had to go through for us. He got all sheepish then and nearly cried; he told me his whole life story and how he'd tried to get into drama school and failed and had ended up doing some university course to please his parents and how he regretted it every day of his life. So then I felt guilty about laying into him, and even more impressed that he managed to be so up all the time when actually he was so disappointed with the way his life had turned out.

Initially I tried to put the whole acting thing right out of my head after that, but when I heard about Dora's evening classes in a local hall I thought I would give it a go. I still had this dream rooted inside me and I could only pretend that it wasn't there for just so long before the longing would start up again. It usually happened when I was watching telly and saw some really great performance. If I saw someone being given a standing ovation or being given an award like an Oscar, I would actually get an ache inside me, like a yearning to be that person, to have all that love and applause directed at me. A bit sad, I know, but that was just the way it was and I didn't fancy going through the whole of my life longing for something and never actually trying to achieve it. I didn't want to end up like Dave.

Mum had been a bit of an inspiration that way, having gone back to study when she was a grown-up. It must have been incredibly hard to do with kids to bring up and a husband who wasn't exactly supportive about that kind of thing. I do sometimes wonder if it was worth the effort when I see the sort of shit she has to put up with at the job her wonderful degree eventually got her, but that's not the point. The point is she had a dream about getting a degree and bettering herself and that I can completely get.

I'd heard that one or two of the actors from the soaps had

been spotted in Dora's classes, particularly younger ones. Most of them were not what Dave and I would have considered 'serious actors' – they were mostly just playing themselves – but still it was a way into the business and I thought it would be fun. I worked out I could just about afford to pay the fees if I cut down on my drinking on Saturday nights and avoided Topshop as much as possible and stopped downloading music.

I auditioned for Dora, but I knew that I would have to have been monumentally crap for her to have turned me down. If she had restricted herself to taking on people who had any chance of making it, she would have been sitting on her own most evenings. We went through the charade of her 'offering me a place' and pretended it was all a pukka drama school. I didn't mention it at home, just pretended I was working evenings. I really enjoyed being there – partly, if I'm honest, because I knew I was the best in the class.

That evening, at the end, Dora asked me to hang on a second as the others went out, chattering, on the usual high that the whole thing gave us all. Drama classes are great therapy when you're feeling a bit down, brilliant for taking you out of yourself. The two visitors were still huddled in the corner, blowing their noses and talking in low voices, avoiding everyone's eyes.

'I want you to meet someone, Steffi,' Dora said, taking me over. 'This is Tom and Audrey, they're the casting directors for *The Towers*.'

I don't think I actually believed her for a moment. I mean, *The Towers* was the biggest soap in the country. All my life I'd been watching it and reading about the actors who starred in it. In fact, it was really a bit sad how addicted I was to the whole thing. I felt like I knew all the characters personally, as well as all the actors who played them. It didn't seem possible that these two tatty old specimens were part of the world of glittering awards ceremonies and titillating tabloid scandals that were all part of *The Towers*' world. When I'd talked to Dave about my addiction to the series once, he suggested that I liked it so much because it reflected my own life on the estate.

'Fuck off,' I scoffed, 'do you really think life on the estate is that exciting? There's about three murders a week in *The Towers*, we're lucky if we hear of one mugging.' For some reason he thought that was incredibly funny, which gave me the right hump.

'We're looking for a young girl to be part of a new family moving into the area,' the woman called Audrey was saying.

'You mean into the Goddards' flat?' I said, slightly giving the game away that I was an avid fan when I probably should have been trying to show I was a bit cooler.

'Yes.' Audrey smiled rather sweetly at me, which made her look a lot younger. 'You're a fan, then?'

'Yeah.' I think I might have blushed.

'We think you might be great for the part. Would you be interested in coming to the studios to audition?'

'OK.'

OK! That was all I could think to say, and I said it in the flattest, most pathetic little voice. I suppose I thought it would be uncool to jump about screaming and to throw my arms around Audrey and Tom and cover them in kisses and bugger the germs, which was what I really wanted to do. Or maybe I was just frightened that if I once let my excitement out of the box I would never be able to get it back in again, that I would just explode into a million tiny pieces.

Chapter Two

This was a bit of news I wasn't going to be able to keep to myself, no matter how uncool it might seem, and I blurted it out almost the moment I walked through the door that evening. The whole family was there and the noise level hardly faltered; they obviously didn't believe me, or weren't even bothering to listen.

I tried again. 'I've been asked to audition for a part in *The Towers.*'

'Fuck off, Steffi,' Jeremiah, my older brother, said. 'You are such a little liar. Since when do they go talent spotting in hotel kitchens?'

'I've been doing some acting classes and these casting people from the telly company came to watch.'

One or two of them had stopped talking and were taking in what I was saying.

'You're auditioning for *The Towers*?' Mum asked, a puzzled look on her face.

'Over my dead body,' Dad growled and suddenly everyone was silent.

'What do you mean?' I asked, trying to keep the shake out of my voice.

'You've got a perfectly good job, you don't need to do that rubbish.'

'Steffi might end up a star,' one of my little sisters piped up – Jenny, I think. The girls were beginning to get the idea. 'That would be so cool. She'd be able to get us into clubs for free and stuff.'

'And have every slimy newspaper reporter in the world sniffing through our bins looking for stories,' Dad exploded. 'No thank you.'

'There's nothing to be ashamed of in my bins,' Mum protested, which made some of them laugh and sort of defused things a bit, although Dad's face was still like thunder.

'OK.' I shrugged, having no intention of causing a major row. 'I probably wouldn't have got it anyway.'

'Oh, that is so unfair,' Jenny squeaked. She was always the bravest at speaking up when Dad was in a mood – for some reason she got away with more than the rest of us. 'I wish someone would ask me to be in *The Towers*. You'll be a celebrity and everything.'

'I don't want to hear any more about it,' Dad bellowed, making even Jenny cower. 'We are a respectable family and we don't want to have anything to do with that sort of thing.'

I didn't intend to make a big fight of it – not yet, not when there was still a chance I wouldn't get the job anyway – but I didn't intend to miss the opportunity to go to the studios either. It was like an invitation to step into my own magic kingdom, instead of just having my nose pressed to the screen, so to speak; I would actually be able to walk among my heroes

14

and heroines – just thinking about it had made me come over all Shakespearean.

★   ★   ★   ★

Dora, being the wily old bird again, had realised I didn't have the faintest idea how to get to the studios, since they were right over the other side of London in some suburb I'd never heard of, and she had offered to drive me there. It was kind of her, don't get me wrong, but I knew she really wanted to be there herself because she got as much buzz out of the thought of hanging out with the stars as I did. She might put on this act of having seen it all and done it all, but if they had offered her the part of an old bag lady she would have been down on all fours kissing their feet. I knew that and she knew I knew. We had a bit of an unspoken understanding, Dora and me.

When I got to her flat the next day I hardly recognised her. She'd even washed her hair instead of just piling it on top of her head and sticking it together with pins, and she was wearing make-up, which actually looked a bit spooky, like a small child had painted a woman's face on her. Her car was a pretty good disaster. I doubt if she had ever removed a single piece of rubbish from it in all the years she'd owned it and it reeked of old fag butts, which upset me a bit since I'd spent about an hour in the bathroom that morning, before anyone else was awake, trying to make myself smell like a meadow in springtime.

'Just be yourself,' she kept saying as we drove, which seemed pretty rich coming from someone who looked totally unlike her usual self. 'They'll love you.'

'OK.'

Funnily enough, I wasn't nervous about the actual audition, but I was excited at the thought of maybe meeting some of the cast and seeing what things were like inside a real television studio.

'I feel like Alice Through the Looking Glass,' I told her, 'about to step through the screen into a world of make-believe.'

'You've read Lewis Carroll?' she asked, obviously surprised.

'Nah,' I laughed, 'I saw it on telly one Christmas. Did he write it, then?'

Dora laughed and nodded. I made a mental note to see if I could get a copy. I always tried to do that. If I heard someone talking about a book I would go into a bookshop and ask for it. I never read around the house, that was asking for trouble, but I liked to have a book in my bag for travelling on the bus and for my breaks at work. Everyone at home, apart from Mum, thought reading books was a sign of weirdness. She'd given up trying to persuade them different. Maybe some of the others were doing it on the quiet too, like me. Dave had been useful for recommending stuff. He used to lend me things he'd read and liked as well.

The reception area at the television studios lived up to all my fantasies, with giant blow-ups on the walls from all my favourite programmes and a gigantic glass reception desk with beautiful women in immaculate suits dealing with the visitors. As Dora and I waited to be fetched I scanned every passing face in the hope of spotting someone famous. I was sure I recognised some of them, but it was hard to tell when they just looked like ordinary people going to work.

Everyone seemed to be so busy and it was almost as if we

were invisible. Well, that's not strictly true – it was just me, really. It was almost as if I had vanished, or at least wasn't someone they could talk to directly. Women with clipboards and earphones kept talking to Dora as if I wasn't there.

'Is this Steffi McBride?'

'Does she have an appointment?'

'Does she have an agent?'

Hello? I do have a brain, you know, was what I wanted to say, but I didn't – mainly because I was so thrilled to be there at all, but also because Dora seemed to take it all for granted. It was like she was a farmer bringing her prize young heifer to market, to have her prodded around by potential buyers before they started haggling over a price.

'Should I have an agent?' I whispered, in a moment when they had all gone away again.

'Probably. Certainly if they offer you the job.'

'How do I find one?'

'That won't be hard. I know plenty.'

'Couldn't you do it? You know how all this stuff works.' The idea grew on me. 'Tell them you're my agent. They only seem to want to talk to you anyway.'

'OK.'

She was acting all cool about it, but I could tell she was made up that I'd asked. I was quite happy with the idea because I trusted her, and anyway it was only because of her that I was there at all. I was starting to get even more excited as this woman with an earpiece led us off through loads of corridors. She explained as we walked that they'd already held mass auditions for this part.

17

'They've seen about eighty people,' she burbled, 'done recalls and everything, but they just can't make up their minds. Apparently, they want to build this family up to be a big part of the series, so they're taking the casting really seriously.'

That piece of information certainly didn't do anything to calm my growing nerves.

After that, it all became a bit of a blur. The woman took us through to the studios and there I was, in my own personal Narnia. It was like walking into a gigantic warehouse full of room sets, a bit like Ikea, only the room sets were actually recognisable from the series. There was the Goddards' kitchen, and someone else's sitting room and the local pub. They all looked strangely vulnerable with their missing walls and ceilings. Some of the ones that weren't used so often had been packed up and stored on giant trolleys, labelled with their fictional owners' names. It was like walking across one of those Hollywood back lots you see in the old Fred Astaire movies.

There was a central sitting area where the actors were all lurking around while the technicians and directors and everyone got ready. Everywhere I looked I saw familiar faces from *The Towers*. One or two of the men were quite friendly, a bit lechy if I'm being honest, but most of them seemed to look right through me as though I was invisible again, especially the women. Audrey with the roots was there and she'd scooped up a few actors to do a scene with me; we headed off to a room on the other side of the studio where there was a giant table, like a company boardroom, and we all sat down.

She gave me a script and said I could just read it, I didn't have to learn it – but I read it once and then I was able to chuck it away. For some reason, I've always been able to learn scripts; it's a knack. It's not that I'm bright – quite the opposite, the only GCSEs I got were art and drama – but I just seem to absorb scripts after one read-through. I can do it after one hearing too. I can recite virtually every episode of *Friends* or *Sex and the City*, which drives my sisters mad at home because I say the lines a split second before the characters do when we're watching the DVDs. I just can't help myself. I could even learn the Shakespeare pieces that Dave used to give us. It would drive me insane when the others were still using their books at rehearsals and I was trying to do my Helen Mirren thing and be all professional. It's the same with songs; I hear them once or twice and then I can sing them straight through. Not exactly the most useful skill in the world, but nice to know I can do something.

They gave me some background notes about the character and her family history and how she came to be the person she was. I can't describe how much I loved doing those little scenes that day. The moment I started speaking all my nerves went and I forgot that I was staring at soap stars I'd been watching on the screen since as long as I could remember. I just got so into it, and what made it even better was that I could tell they were all impressed. There hadn't been many moments in my life when I'd impressed people, more often I seemed to disappoint or exasperate them, so those times kind of stuck in my memory. The other actors weren't looking through me any more; they were actually talking to me and looking me in the eye, like I was one of them. The producers had loads of photographs, which I discovered later were of actors they had already cast to be part of the new family. They kept looking at the pictures and then up at me, narrowing their eyes, straining to see if they could imagine a family resemblance.

Audrey and Dora were virtually purring with pleasure on the sidelines and I noticed other cast members were drifting into the room to watch. At the end everyone was gathered around chatting to me, like I was the star and they were the fans. I told Audrey that I wanted Dora to be my agent and Audrey said she would be talking to her the next day. They kept saying that they couldn't promise anything, but they all seemed dead certain I was the one for the part. Dora was certainly acting like it was a done deal.

'What will your boyfriend have to say about all this?' she asked as we drove back across London.

'Pete?' I was shocked to realise I hadn't given him a second thought all day. 'Pete doesn't have much to say about anything really. He'll be cool.'

Pete and me had been together since year ten at school. He was the opposite to me. Whereas I had a Jamaican mum and an Irish dad, he had an Irish mum who worked behind the bar in our local and a Jamaican reggae-singer dad. Pete's dad was the most chilled guy I had ever met, mainly because he was stoned most of the time, and Pete was pretty much following in his footsteps. At school he had been fairly alert, but the more drugs he did and the more into his music he got, the more spaced out he became. I still loved him but I had to admit he was pretty useless for anything except lying around having a laugh. When it came to lying around, Pete was pretty much king of the world.

His dad didn't mind that he was useless – if they were together, they would just make music all the time – but it drove his poor mum insane. She was one of those women who had worked all her life, having to bring up her younger brothers and sisters from when she was ten years old, all that sort of thing, and her feckless Caribbean men drove her bananas. In the end she threw Pete out, guitar, stash and all. Not that it bothered him much because he'd heard of an empty flat on the other side of the estate, so he just broke in there and started a squat, which was handy for me when I was keen to get away from one of Dad's moodies. We'd had some good times round there, and some pretty weird ones too.

It had been a real surprise to me, the day Pete first showed an interest. Up till then I'd hardly been the most popular girl in school. Actually, I'd been pretty unpopular in some quarters and had been getting a spot of bullying from one or two of the 'cool' girls, who thought I was a bit of a geek with the drama and everything. There was this incident on the way home one afternoon when they ganged up on me. I guess they were only fooling around, but it was a bit scary and they knocked my books out of my hands and ran off with them.

I probably would have been more upset if I'd come from the sort of family where everyone was nice and calm and gentle all the time, but I was pretty much used to looking after myself at home anyway. It wasn't nice to be picked on like that; everyone wants to be popular, don't they? But it wasn't the end of the world. Anyway, Pete was walking behind and came up to talk to me, walked me home like a real gentleman. Apparently he'd fancied me for ages but hadn't thought I'd be interested. I was definitely interested, I can tell you, and from that moment on I didn't have any more trouble. It didn't make them like me any more than they had before – in fact, it probably made them like me less, since they all had the hots for Pete – but they couldn't say anything. Being Pete's girlfriend made me untouchable. All they could do was give me looks and suck their teeth at me when I went past without him. If he was there, they would pretend to be my best friends. What was really nice was Pete didn't seem to realise the effect he had on everyone else; he just fancied me and wanted to go out with me.

'Sometimes boyfriends can feel a bit left out of things when something like this happens,' Dora warned.

'Pete is so out of it anyway he won't feel a thing,' I assured her.

Funnily enough, she didn't ask me how my dad would take it. I guess she sort of assumed he would be thrilled that one of his children might get a part in the biggest soap opera on television. Most fathers would be proud, wouldn't they? I hadn't told her about how weird he'd been about the idea of me even auditioning. To be honest, I was still trying to work it out myself.

Even though he'd reacted so badly the night before, I somehow assumed that he would feel differently when he knew I might actually get the job. I mean, soap actresses make a good living, don't they? It's practically a steady job, steadier than washing up in some poxy hotel kitchen and being treated like the lowest of the low by a bunch of complete scumbags.

Should have known better. I waltzed into the flat, all smiles and pleased with myself, unable to keep the news to myself and it turned into World War III. He just yelled and yelled and yelled, accused me of 'putting on airs and graces', 'thinking I was better than the rest of them', 'being a tart'. I mean, for God's sake, when I came home with my obviously stoned and unemployable boyfriend he was as laidback as anything. Suddenly I was a 'tart' for wanting to act on television? Where was the logic in that?

Normally I would just have given in when he put his foot down like this, but there was no way I was giving up this opportunity to live out every dream I had ever dreamed. I didn't scream back at him, but I folded my arms and refused to take any of his crap, until eventually he lost control and went for me. That brought Mum in from the kitchen like an avenging angel. She might have been willing to allow him to lay into her, but he was never allowed to lay a finger on any of us. She was actually wielding a frying pan, like a character from a *Tom & Jerry* cartoon. She held him off me, shouting for me to make a run for it and leave her to deal with him. I didn't like the idea of what he would do to her once I was gone, but then I saw Jeremiah gesturing at me to go.

'I'll look after her,' he said, quietly enough for Dad not to hear. 'You go. He'll calm down once you've gone.'

'Fucking charming,' I thought, once I was outside with the door slammed behind me. 'How did I get to be the baddie all of a sudden?'

There was nothing for it but to go round to Pete's and doss down there for the night. At least there I'd get some serious loving and something decent to smoke. I reckoned I would stay there until Mum gave me the thumbs up to say Dad had calmed down enough for me to go back.

Chapter Three

The next day my whole life changed. Goodbye to the hotel kitchens, goodbye to being paid bugger all, hello to the best job imaginable, starting at fifty grand a year. Fifty grand a year! I couldn't believe it when Dora told me. I mean, fucking hell, that's the sort of money that men in suits and Jaguars earn, isn't it?

'They've sent over the contracts,' she told me when I phoned, 'which I'll go through for you, although I'm sure it's all standard stuff. You start with a three-month contract, with an option for the following three months. And they've sent some scripts too, which you had better come and get.'

She sounded so excited for me it brought tears to my eyes. She was usually such a cynical old bag, but I'd always suspected she'd been putting it on to hide her disappointment, or maybe to deal with the boredom of teaching class after class of talentless tossers. No offence meant.

I went straight over to her flat and she said I could stay there to read the scripts – a relief, because Pete's place was a bit crowded and there was often no electricity, which made everything difficult, and there was no way I could go back home just at the moment unless I was going to grovel to Dad and promise to give up any ideas of becoming an actress. Fat chance of that now! Mum said there was no way he was willing to back down yet, so we had a stalemate and I was going to be on Pete's skanky old mattress for a while yet. I curled up on an old sofa in the corner of Dora's sitting room, which was covered in shawls and cats, and started to read, while she sat at the kitchen table on the other side of the arch reading the contracts and chain-smoking.

My character was called Nikki and, to be honest, she was a bit of a slag. This was not going to be a great stretch for my acting talents. Nikki was on the game, disappearing up the West End the whole time, all glammed up, and then coming home to the family and slopping around the house looking like shit. They wanted this dramatic difference between the two sides of her life. She liked to think of herself as a 'high-class escort', but actually she was just a slapper willing to turn tricks in return for a few quid. She was a 'good-time girl', enjoying her work and sometimes even bringing it home with her. I'd met a few like her over the years on the estate. They were often the most interesting types to us when we were little because they were the ones with the nice clothes and jewellery; at least it seemed nice to us then, although as I grew up and started reading the decent fashion magazines I realised it was all pretty tacky stuff. What I liked about those women was that they didn't care what anyone thought of their morals or anything like that, they just cared about what people thought of their bodies, their nail or hair extensions and their fake tans. They were completely honest about their ambitions and their determination not to get stuck in dead-end jobs until they had to and not to get weighed down with kids and useless husbands who treated them like skivvies and knocked them about whenever they'd had a few too many. If I hadn't had my silly dream about being an actress I probably would have gone much the same route. (Actually, I probably wouldn't, because Dad would have knocked seven bells out of me the first time I tried to go out in fishnets and hair extensions.)

Dora said the buzz around the studio was that they were wanting to stir up a bit of controversy with Nikki, get the media tutting over the declining standards of behaviour among young people and 'the shocking things that get shown on telly these days'. Normally I would have been all for that. I like a bit of shocking behaviour myself, but I could just imagine what Dad's reaction was going to be. This was exactly what he was worried about, me tainting our 'respectable' family name. I felt a tiny stirring of nausea deep inside my stomach, partly because I knew there was no way I wasn't going to play this one to the hilt. If they wanted a slapper, a slapper was what they were going to get, with all the necessary bells and whistles. I would be the sluttiest fucking slapper to hit the small screen since ... well, since forever. But how long would it take for my father to talk to me again? Although I didn't know the details, I knew there had been feuds in his family before that had gone on forever, with people refusing to speak to one another all the way to the grave. I'd never even met his mum and dad and he absolutely refused to talk about them. I only knew they were alive because Mum told me one day when he was out, and then made me promise not to mention them to him.

'But why have they fallen out?' I wanted to know.

'Oh,' she muttered, 'we don't need to know the details. I dare say he has his reasons. Just don't make him angry with your questions.'

I couldn't bear the thought of him and me ending up like that; but, on the other hand, I couldn't bear the thought of turning down this opportunity either. He was the one who was being unreasonable, not me; he just had to be won over.

The contracts were duly signed and, because they had taken so long to find the right person to play Nikki, I was able to start work almost immediately. Going in the first day was like starting at a new school, not knowing where to go or what to do. The dressing rooms were really tatty and rundown, like all the money had been spent on the set and nothing backstage. There was a couch in mine, which took up nearly the whole room, a tiny dressing table and a light with a bare bulb, a bit like a prison cell. My name had been typed on a piece of paper and stuck to the door. I noticed that the more established cast members had their names on little brass plaques and screwed on properly, which made me feel like I wasn't likely to be there for long.

Everyone seemed to be rushing from one set to another and they always seemed to understand what was expected of them next. I'd learned every line of the script religiously, but I still didn't know when to go for something to eat or when I needed to report to Make-Up. The technicians and cameramen were a godsend. I noticed that lots of the other actors didn't talk to them at all, but that made me feel uncomfortable. I discovered that, when a director didn't make it clear what he or she wanted me to do, I could usually find a technician who would point me in the right direction, making sure I was visible to the camera and not blocking anyone else, things like that. If you didn't get things right first time they had to re-shoot, which took time, and everyone always seemed to be in a desperate hurry to move on to the next scene. It was the rush and urgency that made the days exciting, but it was nerve-racking too when you were terrified of letting the others down. There was a definite pecking order among the cast, with the old hands ruling the roost and newcomers like me scratching around at the bottom. I got the feeling that I needed to watch everything I said and not give anyone the idea that I fancied myself; a bit like being back at school in that way too.

A lot of the cast were untrained people like me (sorry, Dora, but it's true really), just able to be themselves. Others were really serious actors who had been to proper drama schools and acted in Shakespeare and at the National and all the serious stuff. They were the ones I really loved to watch at work. They would come into work looking completely different and talking in posh actorish voices; then, as they went through Make-Up and Wardrobe, they would gradually become their characters, their voices and personalities changing so that by the time they were on the set they were unrecognisable. I wanted to be like them. I wanted to be able to transform myself and live in different skins.

Once I'd settled in there wasn't anything about my new job that I didn't love. I loved the rehearsals, the banter in the canteen, the parties at the other cast members' houses or at clubs in the West End, the hours in Make-Up and Costume and even the hours and hours of sitting around on the set waiting for the moment to say a couple of lines. Even though we would be there from seven in the morning till seven or eight at night, six days a week, I never wanted to leave. Some days I didn't even have a scene to do, I just had to be there in case something came up, and to sit in the background in pub scenes or street scenes. The old hands would grumble a bit on those days, but I didn't care. I was happy watching and learning from them. But what I really liked were the big dramatic scenes that were being written in for Nikki. Audrey told me that they'd known I was right for the part when they saw me crying and snotting and telling the story about Mum and Dad fighting. Nikki had lots of scenes like that, although I tried to keep the snot to a minimum, and I loved every minute of them, losing myself completely while the cameras were turning and Nikki was doing her thing.

What I liked most was that I knew they were going down well. Everything would be silent in the studios when I finished and everyone would be watching, even the technicians who usually spent most of their time looking bored, eating sandwiches or scratching themselves. I knew that I could hold people's attention and I couldn't wait for the episodes I was filming to be aired. I was sure that Dad would be so proud of my acting abilities that he would be willing to overlook the fact that I was playing the sort of woman he had so much contempt for, and might actually start talking to me again.

It was going to be six weeks from my first day's filming to the first showing of Nikki on the nation's screens, so by the time the day came it felt like I'd been working there forever. The publicity people had been hard at work as well, getting me interviews in magazines, talking about my favourite night out and 'what I liked most about boys' and other stuff, which was so stupid I could hardly stop myself from laughing out loud. Then there was the fashion shoot, which was something else altogether.

It all came about because I was chatting to one of the women in Make-Up. The women who do those sorts of jobs are so nice. I guess they're pretty good jobs to get if you're into that sort of thing and don't mind mucking about with other people's greasy skins and hair. This woman was working away on doing me up for one of Nikki's nights out on the town and she was telling me about her life. She must have been really old because she had actually made up Twiggy once, and I remembered doing Twiggy in history at school (it's about the only thing I can remember from history lessons). She'd had an amazing time, going all over the world on *Vogue* shoots and the whole bit, and I was pretty impressed.

'Have you ever done any modelling?' she asked.

'Me?' I was genuinely shocked for a second. I mean, I had always been the scuzzy-looking one in our family. Then I realised it was probably something she said to everyone, just polite small talk. 'Nah.'

'You should. You've got great bones. The camera loves you, ask anyone in Production. You should arrange something, Claire.' She had turned her head to talk to another girl sitting on the other side of the room, who I knew was from Publicity.

'Arrange what?' Claire asked.

'Get Steffi a fashion shoot with one of the big magazines. She would be a natural. I'll do the make-up for you. If you get someone to run off some pictures and show a few editors, I bet you'll get interest.'

Claire said, 'Great idea,' and made a note on her clipboard, which I thought was just her being polite, because she was one of those incredibly polite upper-class types. To be honest, I then forgot all about the conversation, because I had a big scene that afternoon which took all my concentration. Everyone was very nice afterwards, the crew even gave me a round of applause – which made one of the older cast members grumble a bit, because I don't think it was really the done thing for someone as new as me. I was actually beginning to get a bit embarrassed by all the praise. I didn't want to make any enemies with the others and I could tell one or two of them were getting tired of being told how brilliant I was. I was still just getting away with it because most of them had realised I was as surprised as they were by the whole thing, but I knew it was only a matter of time before I slipped up and accidentally upset someone by seeming up myself. I was still very aware I was the new girl around the place and I was making a real effort to think before I spoke.

Anyway, a few days later, posh Claire came looking for me and told me she had set up a fashion shoot with *Elle*, one of the glossy magazines. I was a bit taken aback, but didn't say anything, not wanting to seem like I was being unprofessional or anything, and duly turned up at the photographer's studio in Charlotte Street at about five in the morning with a bloody great zit on the end of my nose. The nice woman from Make-Up was already there and assured me she could make the zit disappear. 'And they'll airbrush you to death anyway,' she assured me.

Well, hats off to models. I always thought that whole game was a bit of a doss, but they had me working like a dog right through the day. They had me in positions that were so painful I thought I might never walk straight again and some of the clothes they pinned me into were like medieval torture machines. But I kept up the whole professional, 'don't complain, do whatever you're asked' thing, which I know from reading interviews with models in magazines is what you're supposed to do.

At the end of the day, they showed me some of the pictures, and even before the airbrushing I have to say I was quite shocked. If I had come across them in a magazine I would not have known they were me. I'm not even sure I would have recognised the outfits, which looked like shit in real life but came across in the pictures like sex with stitching. They were incredible pictures – I mean, really incredible. I actually fancied myself in them. I could understand why other girls might dash out to the shops to try to re-create the look, even though I knew the look was hideous in reality, because I would have done that. Once I'd got over the shock I actually felt pretty proud of myself. Even though I knew I didn't really look like the girl in the pictures, it was cool to think that I had managed to achieve 'the look', even if only for a few hours. It had been a bit like another acting assignment.

'We're going to have to get a bit of a grip on this publicity thing soon,' Dora said when I told her about the magazine shoot. 'You should really be getting paid for some of this stuff.'

'Oh, I don't mind,' I interrupted, terrified that she might make a fuss and make them think I was a prima donna. 'I quite enjoy it really, and it's good for promoting the show.'

'Sweet of you to have their interests at heart,' she growled, 'but we mustn't let them exploit you. We won't say anything until you've started appearing on the screens and have built a fan base, then we can start making a few demands.'

'The public may absolutely hate Nikki,' I said, 'in which case I may be looking for another job in a few months.'

'That's not the buzz at the company. They've been making noises about tying you in to a longer contract, although I'm not agreeing to anything like that yet.'

'Why do they want to do that?'

'They think you're going to be a star.'

I couldn't think of anything else to say to that. It was like she'd punched me in the stomach and knocked all the air out of me.

Commuting to work from Pete's grotty squat had proved pretty impossible, and Mum warned me that it still wasn't safe for me to go home just yet, so I'd had to look around for somewhere a bit closer to the studios. There was a cameraman, called Gerry, who I'd got to know quite well in the canteen and from sitting around on set. Cameramen are funny blokes. Sometimes it seems like actors don't exist for them. I suppose they get used to just staring at us through their lenses, thinking of us in terms of light and shade and filling the frame; they forget we're people too. He was good looking in a rugged sort of way, never seemed to take much notice of his clothes or grooming, but I kind of liked that. He didn't even try to hit on

me and it was me who struck up our first conversation. There's
something about the 'strong silent' types that makes me want
to find out what makes them tick. The more enigmatic they
are the more I want to get to the bottom of them. He was
around thirty and had spent the last few years travelling around
the world making documentaries but had moved back home
with his parents since getting the job on *The Towers*. They lived
just a short walk from the studios.

'We've got a spare room you could rent, if you like,' he
offered, as if it was the most natural thing in the world.

'That would be great.' I jumped at the offer. 'I wouldn't be
in the way at weekends, it would just be somewhere to sleep
during the week so I can get in and out of work easily.'

Gerry's family were just so sweet, like something out of a
commercial but thirty years out of date. The house was one of
those semi-detached places and they gave me a thing that was
like a combined alarm clock, kettle and teapot, which woke
me up each morning with a lot of hissing and clanking as it
came to the boil and automatically made a cup of tea. How
cool is that? Gerry's mum was always up and dressed by the
time I came downstairs, happy to cook me breakfast, and his
dad would read bits out of the *Daily Mail*, which they would
discuss and ask my opinion on. They were just the cutest
people and what I really liked was Gerry didn't make any
apologies for how they were, didn't try to show that he was
cooler than they were. He accepted them for what they were,
just as he had accepted me. Some people always seem to want
to change other people rather than just accepting them for
who they are, but Gerry wasn't one of them. Maybe that was

why he was a good cameraman, just watching what went on and recording it rather than trying to influence it like a director might. The whole family were just so peaceful together that when Gerry slipped into my bed in the middle of the night the first time I didn't have the heart to turf him out. He was actually wearing pyjamas, with a cord and flies and everything! It just seemed so easy and natural and comfortable. He made me feel safe and I was grateful to him for being such a good friend.

★   ★   ★   ★

The night that my first episode was being aired I didn't have the nerve to stay in and watch it with Gerry's family, which I think disappointed them a bit, but I just couldn't have stood the embarrassment. I couldn't go to Pete's either, because the electricity supply was so unreliable and I doubted if any of the others there would want to sit through a soap opera even if the telly was working. So I took up Dora's offer of watching it round at her place. Mum rang to tell me that Dad had banned them all from watching it at home, but she and the girls were going to go round to Auntie Pat's. 'Sod him,' she said, 'he can sit in on his own for a few hours and contemplate his sins. I'm not missing this, girl.' Part of me would have liked to have gone round there with them, but there would have been too much noise and I would have wanted to concentrate. And I wouldn't have been able to say anything without sounding like I was really up myself.

Dora had bought a bottle of champagne, bless her, and some snacks from Marks & Spencer, and she had those old-

36

fashioned, flat champagne glasses like they always used in vintage black-and-white movies. My heart was thumping like it was trying to break through my rib cage. I'd seen rushes and all the rest at work, so I sort of knew what I looked like on the screen, but it was different when it was actually out there in the real world, with the familiar voice of the continuity announcer talking about programmes coming later, and then the theme tune that I must have heard three thousand times before, and the story lines that just the night before I had been following along with the rest of the country – and suddenly there was Nikki. And it was her, not me, up on the screen. It didn't feel like me in any way, just like the photos from the shoot. Luckily, she wasn't on the screen that much in the first episode because I probably would have suffocated, since I didn't seem to be able to breathe when she was there.

I didn't dare to look at Dora until the final credits were rolling up and seeing the tears in her eyes set me off crying too. She covered her embarrassment by topping up my champagne glass. In a way it felt like a relief to have got over the hurdle. Nikki was out there now and it was up to the public whether they took to her or not.

My phone peeped that I had a text. It was from Mum. 'I have never been so proud. You are a star!' I was grateful to her for texting and not ringing, because I don't know how I would have reacted to too much praise at that moment. She always did get that sort of thing right, which was why she was so good with the children in the home where she worked.

Dora and I got well plastered that night. She even broke out some hash that she must have been saving since the

Sixties. She had recorded the show and insisted on playing it back, fast-forwarding through the bits where Nikki was off-screen, and giving me a few more acting tips. She didn't lavish me with praise, which I was grateful for, just talked as if it was another day's work, treating me like a professional. I wasn't in any fit state to go anywhere that night, so I dossed down on her couch, which smelled a bit of old ladies and cats.

Pete seemed to be blissfully unaware that anything had changed in my life. Maybe he was pretending not to notice, but I don't think so. I think he really was just not quite firmly enough on this planet. Very few people are able to completely avoid a media flash flood, but Pete was one of them. He didn't watch television or listen to the radio, he never read a newspaper or a magazine, so virtually every 'overnight sensation' that hit the headlines passed him by. I think that was part of the attraction. He seemed to have the soul of a poet, floating above the vulgar hurly-burly of everyday life.

'You all right, babe?' he would enquire pleasantly when I crawled in through the broken window, falling on top of him and a couple of others as they sat on the mattress below, completely unaware that his girlfriend's face was plastered over virtually every paper and magazine on the newsstands, or that in order to reach him I'd had to dodge through a restaurant and out through the kitchens to avoid a photographer who seemed to have decided to stalk me 24/7.

Nikki, it seemed, had struck a chord in the national affections. A journalist on one of the heavy papers wrote a whole long piece comparing her to Elsie Tanner, Melina Mercouri and Catherine Deneuve. Dora had to explain to me that Elsie Tanner was another slapper character who had been the first person to be seen by the public on *Coronation Street*; the other two I knew had played hookers in famous old movies because I'd watched them when Dave was trying to get a foreign-movie club going at the school. He'd decided to start with a season of hooker movies because he thought that would encourage more boys to join the club, which it did, but it also got him closed down by the headmaster after one term. Apparently, some of the parents complained. I happened to know which parents it was, and if they had actually known what their daughters were up to in the evenings they might not have been quite so up themselves about a few art-house films.

The *Elle* magazine fashion spread came out a short time after Nikki first appeared on-screen and the pictures went everywhere. Dora was becoming quite the ruthless businesswoman, making phone calls and holding meetings and shouting at people about me being exploited and how I deserved a slice of the money-making machine that was building up around Nikki. She had managed to get a clause into my contract that allowed me to do advertising work as long as it didn't interfere with my filming schedule. She kept telling me about deals she had set up and the money all seemed to be fantastic, though I didn't really have the time to follow exactly what she was up to. I kept quiet and let her get on with it, just turning up in photographers' studios when I was told. It was all a bit of a laugh, modelling clothes and make-up and whatever, but what I really wanted to do each day was get back to the studio and develop Nikki's character.

The biggest problem with Nikki was that she kept having love scenes. Well, not really 'love', since she was with punters half the time, but I still had to get my kit off and get down and dirty with a varied selection of men. I got over the embarrassment factor after a couple of weeks, but there was still the yuck factor to overcome from time to time. They weren't all old and disgusting, but some of them were. It wasn't so bad sliding into bed and then cavorting around, it was the kissing that was the worst. There's no way out of it, of course, if it's in the scripts, but I would dread hearing the director shouting, 'Tongues, please!' when I was writhing around with yet another bit-part actor I'd only met that morning. I can see why hookers don't like kissing and I did question whether Nikki would be quite so keen to do that sort of thing with punters, but they told me she was confused about where the line was between her professional and personal behaviour. I didn't want to sound like I was being difficult so I just braced myself and got on with it.

I didn't get to see much of Mum and the rest of them because my working hours coincided with Dad's most days and he was still adamant that he wasn't going to have me in the house. Whenever I did have a day off, Dora crammed it full of advertising and promotional work, which was quite nice because it meant I didn't have a chance to brood over how much I missed the family. We met up whenever we could, but if it was in a public place there was always the problem of people staring or coming over and asking for autographs and pictures. It was great to get all the attention, but embarrassing when you're trying to have a proper conversation with your mother or your sisters. It's bloody hard to sign an autograph without feeling like you're 'putting on airs and fecking graces', as Dad would have put it. But to refuse to sign would have looked even worse. Being with them made me feel sad, especially when they had to leave. I just wanted to go back with them, back to my home, to be part of the bickering and the laughing, not be the one left on my own. But no matter how much I missed being with them, nothing would have persuaded me to give up what I was doing.

Whenever I saw them or rang them, the girls were always on at me to take them clubbing. The boys not so much so. I guess the boys didn't think it was cool to be freeloading on their sister, but the girls weren't worried about anything like that. We had to arrange a night when there was no danger Dad would find out where they were, so Mum waited till she knew he was going away for a weekend's fishing with his mates. We met up in the West End and the girls had really gone to a lot of trouble, bless them. They must have been primping and pimping themselves for fucking hours. They sparkled from head to toe and they just could not keep the grins off their faces. I was so proud of them and was looking forward to showing them off around town. We had a couple of cocktails in a bar first, to get us in the mood, and then headed for the velvet ropes of a club I knew they would love. They had all got themselves kitted out with false IDs to get them past the doormen. We were having such a great time.

'Sorry, girls.' The doorman had his hand up behind me, clipping the rope back into place, leaving my sisters on the other side.

'They're with me,' I said.

'Sorry, Miss McBride —' these guys knew their show business '— club policy.'

'They've got ID,' I pleaded.

'It's not the age,' he said, 'it's the look.'

There was some sniggering rising among the queue, people happy to see potential queue-bargers brought down to size. The girls' little faces broke my heart. People were starting to take pictures with their phones and I knew that if I made a fuss this could be a big story and their humiliation would be a hundred times worse.

'OK, girls,' I said, as breezily as I could, 'let's go somewhere else. This place ain't so fucking great anyway.'

We stalked off into the night, feeling a hundred pairs of eyes on our backs. None of us felt like chancing a second rejection, so we parted in a bit of a chilly atmosphere and they headed home. The story made it into enough papers for them to be well and truly humiliated at school the following week and they never asked me for anything after that. In fact, they hardly ever called me at all — it always had to be me calling them — and then they would act all off-hand, like I was bothering them all the time. I could understand that, after what had happened, but it still didn't feel nice.

'They'll come round,' Mum assured me when I told her what had happened. 'They're young and they've had their pride dented. Just give them a little time.'

I knew she was right, but I was frightened that with my increasingly hectic schedule I might not have the necessary time to keep our relationships going without a bit of help from them. It felt like I was drifting further and further from the family and the tone of the press stories about the rejection outside the club made me nervous. It was as if the journalists were pleased to see me and my family being taken down a peg or two. It was nothing terrible in the great scheme of things, just gentle teasing really, but it seemed like a warning of what might be to come if anything went seriously wrong. It was like I was sailing out to sea in a little dinghy, having no idea what sort of storms might lie ahead and not having my family there for back-up if I got into trouble. I stepped up the work schedule to stop myself from brooding on it.

Chapter Four

'OK,' Dora said, 'here's the deal. You need to buy yourself a house. I've been on to *OK!* and they're willing to pay two hundred thousand for the exclusive rights to photograph you moving in, and they'll furnish it for you and do it up.'

'You're joking me, aren't you?' I was trying to take it all in. 'A magazine is basically willing to pay me enough to buy a house, just for the rights to photograph me in it?'

'Well, you may have to get a mortgage for a bit more than that, but nothing that we can't manage from your salary.'

'I don't know, Dora, do I want the responsibility of a house? I'm not very good at all the paperwork and stuff.'

'You just leave all that to me. You can't go on sleeping on other people's sofas and God knows where else forever. I'm sure your career will keep going now, but if it doesn't you don't want to have wasted this opportunity to get a roof over your head. If *The Towers* was axed tomorrow, you might not work again for years.'

'Shit, really?' When she put it like that, I could see what she was getting at.

'Think of the advantages. You could have your mum and the rest of them round to visit whenever you wanted. You could get some privacy after a hard day's work. You might even get yourself a proper boyfriend.'

I let that one pass. I was well aware that Dora was not a big fan of Pete's, but she had only met him once and she had never seen how sweet he could be when we were alone together; well, alone apart from the others in the squat. The one time they'd met he'd wandered into an interview I was doing in a hotel. I'd told him I'd meet him afterwards in the pub next door, but he got impatient and came looking for me. He was being a bit lairy, feeling out of his depth I guess, and had obviously had a few drinks, which never brought out his nicest side. When Dora politely asked him to wait until I'd finished, he got all arsey and accused me of giving the journalist a blow-job or something. Luckily the journalist was a decent bloke and didn't put any of that in the article. If it had been one of the tabloids, we would have been in serious trouble.

Dora gave me a big talking-to afterwards, told me he was a liability and all the rest. I knew she was right, but you can't just chuck someone because they're a bit of a hopeless case, can you? Not when you love them.

I don't know what I would have done without Dora. I mean, I know she was going to be getting ten per cent of whatever I earned, but that wasn't exactly a fortune, and she seemed to be willing to take over my whole life, like a replacement mother.

'I feel really bad about asking you to do so much for me,' I told her. 'But I just don't seem to have time for anything.'

'Don't worry,' she brushed aside my worries, 'when you're making a fortune I'll be getting my pound of flesh.'

'But you do much more than anyone else's agent.'

'Listen, kid,' she said. 'I've been in this shitty business for nearly half a century, ever since my mother dragged me to my first ballet class. You are by far the most talented person I have come across in all those years. I'm enjoying being the wind beneath your wings, as the song goes. Don't look a gift horse in the mouth – and that's all the clichés you're getting out of me today.'

So that shut me up. I just gave her a hug, which reminded me how long it had been since I'd been able to hug any of the members of my family when I wanted to. I'd hugged Pete a couple of nights before, but he'd been unconscious on something so he didn't exactly reciprocate. Thank God for Dora, that's all I can say.

She found me a nice little terraced house not far from Gerry and his family, so I would still be able to drop in for meals now and then after a hard day at the studios, and the deal with *OK!* was all set up. I felt strangely sad about leaving Gerry's family, almost like I was leaving home again. Gerry was so incredibly cool about it. I'd been afraid he'd get difficult and try to dissuade me – after all, he'd basically had sex on tap with me there – but he never said a word, quite happy to fit in with my plans. We would still spend most of our days together at the studio and he didn't seem to mind whether we slept together or not – which was a bit insulting in one way, but really restful in another. He was a hard one to figure out, which was partly why I stayed interested, I guess.

The décor and furniture that the magazine supplied weren't exactly what I would have chosen – they'd pimped it

up to be a bit 'footballers' wives', to be honest – but it was
another gift horse that didn't need its dentures checking.

The photoshoot was a major embarrassment, and I just had
to grit my teeth and keep telling myself that they were
basically giving me a house and the agony would soon be
over. I had to drape myself around the furniture, trying to
look funky and sexy at the same time, which was more of a
test of my acting than anything I'd ever had to do on any stage
or in front of any camera. They filled the place with flowers,
which was nice of them, even if they did take them away with
them again at the end of the day. They even brought in a fluffy
kitten that I had to pretend was mine, since I didn't have a
celebrity boyfriend I could show off to them. I didn't tell
them about Pete in case they actually suggested I brought him
along. He definitely wouldn't have been the sort of image
they were looking for, and he most likely would have been
laughing too much at the whole set-up to get any pictures
done anyway.

Once they'd all gone, including the kitten, I ordered in a
pizza and opened a few beers and for a while it felt really nice
to have a place of my own. Then I felt a bit lonely, so I rang
Mum to see if she and the girls fancied coming over. About
two hours later they all turned up because Dad had gone
down the pub. I thought it would be really fun, like it had
been when we were all living together at home, but they were
all a bit weird. Mum was really sweet, saying how well I was
doing and how proud she was of me, and the others were
impressed by the place and spent the whole time playing with
the electronics, but none of them really relaxed. They seemed

completely different, like they were on a day out somewhere where they had to behave themselves, like they had to be polite to me because I had invited them to my home.

I was shocked by how scruffy they looked alongside everything in the house, which was all so gleaming new and shiny, and that immediately made me feel guilty for looking down on them. I really wanted them to relax and make some mess around the place, like a proper party, but it ended up all being a bit embarrassing and they all went home at about midnight, even though I said they could stay and sleep on the sofas and stuff. I couldn't understand quite what had happened and I felt bad for the rest of the night.

I tried asking Mum if she thought that Dad would come round to forgiving me soon and if I would be able to come home again to hang out with them. I noticed her eyes were suddenly tearful, but she made a big effort to stay cheerful and suggested I just 'give him a bit longer to get used to everything'. It felt like there was something else going on that she wasn't telling me, but I couldn't think of the right questions to ask to get it out of her.

I missed Mum more than any of the others. Sometimes I would ring her twenty times a day, just to say 'hi' and find out some of the gossip.

'Are you all right, Steff?' she asked on one call I was making during a break in filming, while the lighting people were taking a bloody age to get the shadows right and I was afraid that if I didn't distract myself I would end up eating all the way through the bag of doughnuts Gerry had just given me.

'Yeah, I think so, why?'

'There's this rumour the girls found in a magazine, about you being anorexic, that's all.'

'Fucking hell, Mum, you know how much I eat. How could anyone eat a ton of chips a day and have a fucking eating disorder? You saw me a few days ago, did I look thin?'

'That's what I told them, but they showed me the picture and you do look a bit skinny. The last few times we've seen you you've been wearing all those baggy clothes and I always worry.'

'You don't have to worry about that. What magazine was it?'

She couldn't remember the name of the magazine so after work I popped into the newsagent on the way home, which is always a bit embarrassing when everyone is staring and it's obvious you're looking for stories about yourself. Anyway, I didn't have to look for long – the story was everywhere, illustrated with the same bloody picture. I grabbed an armful of magazines, paid for them, trying to smile politely as the woman behind the till went through the whole double-take thing of working out who I was, and then telling me – like I didn't know already – and I scuttled home to study the stories in more detail.

Not that it was that easy to get in through my own front door, as there were photographers everywhere, all flashing away and shouting questions. I was wearing an old tracksuit that I always pull on after work. It's not the most flattering of items and it helps to distract people from recognising me. It's really comfortable and I love it, but it isn't exactly the item I would have chosen to put on if I'd known I was going to be photographed. Call me vain, but I would prefer not to have to see myself all over the papers looking like some pikey housewife who's given up the battle of life. Unable to think of any other strategy, I tucked my chin into my chest, covered as much of my face as possible with the magazines and made a dash for it, ignoring their shouts.

'Hey, Steff, over here!'

'You all right, Steff?'

'How much do you weigh, Steff?'

'Show us a bit of leg, girl!'

'What you having for dinner?'

'Over here, Steff, over here!'

'Don't be a bitch, Steff!'

I hate being rude to anyone and generally if a photographer or a fan shouts something out in the street I will always try to give a friendly, cheerful answer, but that evening I'd been caught off balance. I didn't know what to say to them and I was slightly afraid I might burst into tears if I tried to fake some cheerfulness, which would give them exactly the sort of picture they needed to confirm that I was having some sort of mental breakdown.

Once I'd got inside, pulled the curtains, had a couple of drinks and calmed down enough to think about it, I realised the picture they were all talking about must have come from the day of the big fashion shoot, although it wasn't one that *Elle* had used in the end. I was wearing this really skimpy outfit, which showed off my legs and arms, and I was lying in a position that made all my ribs stick out. But even taking all that into consideration, it didn't look right. Despite all the eating that I do, I am reasonably skinny, always have been, apart from the boobs – fast metabolism or something – but this was more than that. I had to admit I did look a bit of a bag of bones, but I couldn't quite work out why.

All the writers in the magazines were saying they were worried about me and it was sweet of them to care. I even pulled off my tracksuit bottoms and stared at my legs in the full-length bedroom mirror to check I wasn't missing anything. If anything, they looked a bit chubbier than usual to me – oh my God, was that how it started? Was I deluded? I could remember a girl at school who used to do the whole eating-disorder thing. She looked like a matchstick but she was convinced she was grossly fat. Was my brain playing the same tricks on me? But what about the doughnuts, and the bacon sandwich this morning and the pizza in the canteen at lunch? I hadn't been sticking my fingers down my throat to get rid of that lot, so they must still be in there somewhere. My God, wasn't there a Mars Bar after lunch as well? Yes there was!

The more I stared at the picture, the more I realised that it had been tampered with. Someone had shaved a few more inches off my thighs and my upper arms with an airbrush, or whatever it is they use. And it looked like they might have increased the shadows under my ribs as well. It was done so subtly it was impossible to tell, but I knew what a good job they had done with my zits, so I could believe it was possible.

I could see why Mum might be a bit worried, but at the same time it was quite a sexy image, mainly because it didn't look much like the real me, more like some perfect fighting-goddess fantasy woman off a computer game for boys. 'Fucking hell,' I thought, 'who needs to diet when the photographers can do this for you?'

All the same, I knew it wasn't good. I didn't want young girls going off and starving themselves in order to look like Nikki when even I didn't look like this. It was a bit of a liberty. So I rang Dora.

'I'm ahead of you, darling,' she drawled. 'I've been on to the photographer's people and given them hell, but they deny all knowledge of how it got out there. I've rung the editors who've printed the picture and none of them is saying where it came from. Maybe it was just some guy with a computer out to make a fast buck.'

'I don't want everyone thinking I'm sick,' I grumbled.

'This happens to every young actress at some time,' Dora replied, trying to calm me down. 'They'll change their tack and start printing pictures showing you're putting on weight and "letting yourself go" next.'

'Charming.'

'Goes with the territory. At least they're talking about you. It's when they stop that you have to worry.'

'S'pose so.'

I wasn't so sure that it was right that I should have to put up with this sort of treatment. I mean, I was enjoying the whole celebrity lifestyle, like when I would go to a club and would be ushered straight into the VIP section, but I didn't have that much opportunity to do that sort of thing. By the time I'd got home, made myself some dinner and learned my lines for the next day, I was pretty much ready to drop off, which was pissing Pete off quite a bit. But he could sleep all day, so he was fresh as a daisy by ten o'clock and ready to boogie the night away, as I kept telling him. He always had stuff that would help me overcome the tiredness, but I didn't want to be doing that sort of thing too often. I'd seen how quickly it would start to have an effect on people. I didn't want to end up looking 50 before I was even 25. It was the work I really enjoyed and I didn't want the executives at the studio reading these stories and thinking I was going to be a problem. Dora had always stressed how important it was for an actress to be reliable and if they thought I was going to be off in rehab the whole time they might decide that Nikki should meet with a prematurely sticky end.

'It's possible that it's the studio PR people who are putting the rumours about,' she suggested. 'They like it when their stars get into the papers. It boosts ratings. If another half a million people tune in to *The Towers* to see how skinny you are, they're more than happy.'

'Half a million people?' I was having trouble getting my head round this.

'I'm just guessing. But you used to be a fan, you know how it is.'

It seemed odd to think that just a few months earlier I would have been reading these stories, watching the programme and then going into work the next day to gossip about what I'd seen with a load of other people who didn't have the slightest idea what was really going on. From this side of the looking glass, everything looked so different.

'Yeah, s'pose so. Need to give it some thought. Should I issue a statement or whatever it is people do when they want to deny something?'

'I think a dignified silence might be more appropriate at

this stage. Don't want to make it look like you're "protesting too much".'

'That Shakespeare,' I thought, 'has a little something to say for every occasion.'

'I was going to ring you this evening about something else,' Dora went on. 'Am I right in thinking you can sing?'

'Yeah,' I said.

I've never thought there was any point in false modesty. I hate people who know they're really good at something but have to go through the whole charade of pretending they aren't until someone else comes forward and speaks up on their behalf. I don't think it's big-headed or anything to say I can sing, because it's not like I've done anything to make myself good at it. I just happen to have been born with a good ear and a voice to match.

'There's a production company that's putting together a singing talent competition thing for celebrities. They're going to pair each of you up with professional singers and have them mentor you and do duets and stuff. It's got a prime Saturday-night spot, so it would be good exposure.'

'At least people would be able to see I wasn't anorexic,' I said.

'Exactly. And it wouldn't hurt to show them you can sing, in case a West End show came up later on.'

'Really?' I liked that idea.

'Never say never.'

It was a couple of days before I heard from her again.

Chapter Five

'Luke Lewis?' I could hardly find the breath to speak. 'You're kidding.'

'Why, is that a problem?' Dora asked.

'No, it's not a problem. Well, yes, actually it might be.'

I'd only been in love with Luke Lewis for around five years, from when I was about 12 till I was at least 17, and when I say 'in love' I mean the whole weeping, screaming, tearing my hair out and hanging around outside stage doors passion. He was lead singer with West End Boys, who were just the most beautiful boy band that ever existed. I read somewhere they had more number-one hits than Take That, Boyzone or Westlife, I mean they were immense. During those five years I would have died for Luke if he'd asked me, but fortunately he never asked. In fact, he never even saw me, walked right past my outstretched fingers every time I managed to get to the front of the pack. I never once managed to catch his eye from the stage, no matter how loudly I screamed his name. I even tried fainting at a concert once, but I just got carted off by some smelly middle-aged biker who insisted that I needed to have my clothing loosened and gave me a drink of water, which meant I'd lost my place in the front row by the time I got back.

'I had a bit of a crush on him when I was a kid,' I confessed.

'Oh, well, now you'll have a chance to live out all those fantasies, because he's going to be your partner.'

The celebrity singing show had become a reality. I'd been for a sort of audition, although they weren't that bothered whether the celebrities involved could sing or not since they were just as happy to have us make fools of ourselves in front of millions of people as to knock 'em dead. I could see they were quite surprised by my voice, which was a nice feeling, and once they'd realised I could sing they had sort of lost interest in the audition and talked more about the format of the show and the publicity they wanted to rev up around it.

I quite liked the idea of the publicity because the anorexic story seemed to be running and running. Other pictures had appeared with bits of me airbrushed out, but the more I tried to point that out to journalists who asked, the more it sounded like I was covering something up. I was accusing the media of faking the stories, and they couldn't accept that, so the myth just kept on growing, even though they could see the truth with their own eyes when they interviewed me or watched Nikki taking her kit off on telly (which she did most nights of the week, what with repeats and omnibus editions and everything). I was beginning to see how the newspapers worked. Once they found a story that their readers were interested in they did everything they could to keep it going, just like our scriptwriters would keep a plot line going for as long as they could, only changing it when the public showed signs of getting bored.

Every journalist in the world seemed to have decided they

wanted to be my mother, even the men, and they were all writing articles telling me what I should be eating and how I should be handling my fame and my career, worrying that I was getting too much success too soon and wouldn't be able to handle it. I couldn't understand how so many people I had never met could have so many opinions about me. I only had one opinion about them: I thought they should all shut the fuck up. As far as I could see, my 'successful' career consisted of remembering to set the alarm clock each morning and making sure I knew the lines by the time the cameras were rolling. We were doing three new episodes a week and Nikki was in virtually all of them, so, when you added on the other jobs Dora was cramming in, I didn't have time for anything – including reading most of the magazines and articles, thank God.

I asked Pete if he thought I was too thin and he got that sort of glazed, puzzled look he gets with most of the questions he's asked. It's not that he's thick or anything, it's more like the drugs have rearranged everything he's ever learned in his head and he has trouble laying his hands on the right file when he needs it. Bless him.

'Do you think I'm too fat?' I asked again in a silly momentary panic.

'Jesus, give me a break,' he wailed, as if I was always nagging him with my questions. I honestly think it was the first time I'd ever raised the subject with him.

Mum was as scornful of the stories as I was, but she still kept turning up with extra food, and would then sit around the kitchen watching me as I ate it. I didn't protest because it was nice to have her there and it gave us a chance to catch up on the family gossip. The one subject we both seemed to spend most of our time avoiding was Dad. If I did mention him I could see a look in her face that was somewhere between panic and misery and I didn't want to put her through that when we had so little time together, so I steered clear of it.

When the production company for the singing competition asked me to nominate a charity to donate my prize money to, should I win, I put forward the children's home that Mum worked in – because you never know with charities just where the money would go, do you, but I knew Mum would keep an eye on it. She'd talked about 'her kids' to us so often over the years that I almost felt like I knew them all personally. One or two of them had come to the house for Sunday lunch from time to time, or to stay for a night or two once they turned 18 and the system turfed them out on to the street. They never stayed long because Dad would make his views very clear on how he felt about putting a roof over the heads of other people's kids, 'when I have enough trouble affording a roof over my own kids' heads'. Once or twice Mum put up a fight about it, but mostly she would just smile and secretly slip them a bit of money before sending them off into the world on their own.

Now, even more bizarre than the anorexia story, the magazines and papers also had me down as a 'fashion icon'. Not only was it weird that they were all telling me I was too thin, but at the same time they were telling their readers that they should try to dress like me. It was doubly weird, because

I hadn't bought any new clothes since God knows when. Firstly, I didn't have that much spare money yet, as Dora was still getting all that side of things sorted out, but more importantly I didn't have the time to go shopping. If you're filming all day, and people are staring at you whenever you go out to the shops, you can't really spend a couple of hours wandering around Topshop with any comfort. So I'd just been wearing all the things I had collected up till then, the same sort of stuff I would wear when hanging out at the squat with Pete, like cheap little dresses over jeans, second-hand jumpers, Oxfam bargains, all the usual stuff. But the fashion editors seemed to think it was a genuine look that I was cultivating. I kept appearing in their 'best-dressed' lists and they would have arrows pointing to various items, telling the readers where to get them (and they never seemed to get that right either). I liked the fact that people thought I looked good in my clothes, but I was a bit spooked by the thought that little girls might believe what they read and would actually spend their hard-earned Saturday-job money trying to reproduce a look that should have been more or less free.

'You're thinking about it too much,' Dora said when I voiced my fears. 'They'll turn on you soon enough and you'll find you're on the "worst-dressed" lists instead. Just enjoy it while it lasts.'

The good part of it was that I started to get invites to go to fashion shows and some of the shops would give me free stuff. I hardly ever wore any of it, because it was nearly always awful, but I would give it to other people at work or ask Mum to pass it round at home.

'You were always the one for dressing up,' Mum chuckled happily one day when I was handing over some of my freebies for her to give to my sisters. 'I remember when I used to come home and find you had turned out all my cupboards and would be strutting round the house in my high heels and scarves.'

I remembered that so well. I would spend hours playing with clothes, dressing my little sisters up like dolls. Mum used to have drawers full of brightly coloured Caribbean scarves and materials that could be twisted round our little bodies into exotic dresses and piled up on our heads as turbans as we paraded around, making up characters and acting them out in stories which were always the same. I used to play with the girls a lot in those days, when they were still young enough to do whatever I told them. I would construct plays – with me in the leading roles, naturally. I was the big star, they were happy to be the chorus girls, obeying my directions. Once they started to complain that they wanted to have their share of the limelight I lost interest. Gradually, I had found myself becoming distanced from them; they got friends and interests of their own, none of which held my attention. I started to like it better playing inside my own head, or lying in front of the television, drinking in the films and soaps and music videos like my life depended on it. Mum would worry sometimes that I didn't seem to socialise like the others, didn't like hanging around in big groups. She seemed to think it wasn't natural for a young girl to spend so much time with her own thoughts.

'You're a funny one, you are,' she'd say, but always with

affection in her voice and a twinkle in her eye. I always took comments like that as compliments.

Now that I was getting my head round the idea of the singing programme I was beginning to think it might be a really good thing. (And not just because it meant I could spend time with Luke Lewis.) Maybe it would bring Dad round a bit. I could understand why he didn't like the idea of his daughter being portrayed as a hooker three times a week for all the world to see, even though I didn't think it was a reasonable thing to make a fuss about, but surely he couldn't complain if I was just singing songs? He was always really encouraging when I was in the school choir and all that stuff. Maybe this would be my chance to get back into his affections. He actually cried at Mum's brother's wedding when I stood up at the reception and sang 'Ben', that Michael Jackson song about a rat. I can't have been more than eight but I managed to make most of the people in the room water up. Mind you, half of them were either completely bladdered or stoned by that stage and probably would have cried at anything. I remember it helped to calm down the atmosphere a bit because there'd been a few fights just before that.

I know this is going to sound pathetic, but on the day I was due to meet Luke Lewis for the first time as a grown-up I felt as nervous and star-struck as I would have been when I was 12. His career hadn't exactly been going great guns over the previous couple of years. He hadn't disappeared from sight altogether, but he certainly hadn't had a solo hit since the group had disbanded – none of them had. He was the only one whose name and face were still known to the public at all. It's hard to exaggerate just how beautiful he was when he was a teenager. He was six years older than me and seemed to be the perfect male specimen as far as I and a few hundred thousand other pre-pubescent girls were concerned. Looking back now, I can see he was still pretty girly himself at the time, but we liked that. When you're 12 you don't fancy having your face ripped to pieces with stubble or any of those other smelly, manly realities that we all get a taste for later on. At that stage we just want boy equivalents of ourselves, eyeliner and all.

I'd seen him on telly a few times since then and I knew he was still a bit pretty for someone on the way to thirty, but he was certainly still a looker, and he still had a voice that made me tingle between the legs, reminding me that for five years he was the only man I ever fantasised about. Although I had often seen him live, I had never really taken in how tall he was until he walked into that studio, strode over and shook my hand like it was an honour for him to meet me rather than the other way round. He was well over six foot tall and broadly built – I've always liked that in a man, it makes me feel safe, like they could wrap me up in their arms and protect me from all the dangers of the world.

He'd always seemed really nice when he was interviewed as well, all polite and modest and sweet. I knew he was a bit posh because I'd read virtually every bit of magazine biography that had ever appeared about him. He'd even been to a private boarding school, which sounded like living on another planet as far as we were all concerned at my school, but he never seemed up himself. I think his whole band had met at the same school, although I was aware that might just be a story put about by the media. I was beginning to get the hang of how the whole thing worked on this side of the 'looking glass'. At least, I thought I was.

That first day in the studio, where we would be recording our first song for the competition, I think the producers were hoping we would be really crap together so they could show how much we had improved by the end of the series, or whatever their game plan was. I wasn't nervous about the singing because I knew I would be able to do that, but what if I said something really stupid to him? Or what if he remembered my face from all those times I stalked him? How embarrassing would that be?

He was so polite. When he shook my hand I immediately had to apologise because it was all sweaty, making up some stupid story about having to run for the bus, when he knew perfectly well I'd been picked up from home by a driver in an air-conditioned Mercedes. I think he even gave a little bow of the head at the same time as holding my hand while I babbled stupidly on, but I may have imagined that – having a bit of a Jane Austen moment. He was dressed in that sort of preppy way that posh boys sometimes do: chinos and coloured shirts, jumper round the shoulders, anyone for tennis? That sort of thing. He was just gorgeous, even more gorgeous than I remembered from the days when he had a mop of hair spiked up all over the place and dressed like some Brighton art-student junkie.

'I'm a great fan,' he said, still holding on to my hand and I thought I was going to pass out. I mean, I had been just about to say exactly the same line to him and now I had nothing else lined up to say, so I grinned and laughed like some half-witted hyena.

'Do you know what the first song they've chosen for us is?' he asked, leading me by the hand over to the coffee and croissants.

'No,' I said. 'Is it something really naff?'

'No,' he said. 'It's beautiful. "Summer Wine". Do you know the Nancy Sinatra/Lee Hazlewood version? They did it on their album *Nancy and Lee*. The Corrs covered it in a live recording with Bono as well. It's a beautiful song.'

Who the fuck was Lee Hazlewood? I knew something about Nancy Sinatra, what with her dad and the Rat Pack and everything. I knew the Corrs, but they weren't exactly the sort of thing Pete and I listened to most of the time.

'I've got it on my iPod,' he was saying, fiddling about with the dial and slipping one earphone into my ear and the other into his own. This guy was really into his music. I liked that. Lee Hazlewood's voice wasn't unlike Luke's, although maybe a bit more gravelly. He was right, it was a beautiful song and I knew it was going to be well within my range, which was a relief. I was beginning to have the best time.

A few of the other celebrities were there as well, although I didn't recognise most of them. One was a newsreader. There was a rugby player, who was very sweet, and a woman who had a programme about gardening or something. Most of them were older. I only recognised about half of the singing mentors as well. Luke was by far the most famous as far as I was concerned.

There was a cameraman circling around the crowd, recording us all getting to know one another. I was getting so used to having cameras around by then I hardly noticed. To be honest, I was too busy staring at Luke like some lovesick puppy to really notice anything else. Thinking back now, I suppose the cameraman did stick around us more than the others, so maybe they thought Luke was the most famous one there too, and I was the only person from *The Towers*, which was the top-rated show by miles at the time, so I guess we were the most likely to pull in the viewers. It's so weird how easily I'd got used to things like that – like it was the natural place for me to be in life – forgetting that it was only a few months since I was working the hotel dishwashers.

They took Luke and me into a separate studio to try the song out, just with a backing track, no musicians. The first run-through was a bit bumpy, only because I was so unfamiliar with the words, but even so it was obvious that it was going to work like a dream. The producers and other behind-the-scenes guys were all huddling in small groups, whispering among themselves and glancing over at us.

'I think they might be changing their plans a bit,' Luke said quietly.

'What do you mean?'

'I don't think they realised quite how good you were going to be. It's dawning on them they have a potential megastar on their hands and they're just working out the best way to milk the most money from the situation.'

It's not often I'm completely lost for words, but that was definitely one of those rare occasions. He was so cool about everything and I was trying to be the same, but all I wanted to do was tear his clothes off.

67

Chapter Six

Pete and I were just chilling at his squat the following Sunday afternoon when my mobile went off. It's a number that hardly anyone has, so I hadn't bothered to turn it off, even though we'd been having sex and hadn't wanted to be disturbed. There were other people in there, as always, old school friends of ours, but they were more or less unconscious in the other room listening to music. When I say friends of 'ours', they were more Pete's friends really, people who put up with me because I was with him but wouldn't have given me the time of day otherwise. Someone had managed to get some regular electricity into the place, which made it much more civilised, and warm enough to be able to take your clothes off.

I liked those quiet moments with Pete, partly because they'd become so rare, what with my filming schedules and Pete's sleeping habits. When he was mellow he was lovely to be with. I'd had to disguise myself in the tatty tracksuit, with my hair scraped up inside an old woolly hat of Mum's that looked like a tea cosy, in order to get to the flat without being noticed. It's no good complaining all the time about not being able to go anywhere without being stalked by the paparazzi and then waltzing out the front door in a little Versace number, a pair of Manolos and hair extensions. If you make yourself look ordinary enough, not many people will spot you; they're all too busy getting on with their own lives, worrying about their own problems. Usually it's the photographers who spot you first, and that attracts everyone else's attention, which is really embarrassing. All you want to do is make them go away before anyone notices, but if you ask them to fuck off they just act like they can't hear you and keep snapping away.

As we had been a bit wild about shedding our clothes it took me a while to find the tracksuit bottoms the phone was in. I got there just in time before it stopped ringing, but in too much of a rush to check the name before picking up. If I'd known it was going to be Luke I probably wouldn't have chosen to take the call while I was stark naked and still pretty sweaty from having been a bit athletic.

'Oh. Hi,' I said, scrabbling to find a voice that wouldn't raise Pete's suspicions that I was being rung by another man before I'd had a chance to explain, but would still sound friendly and welcoming to the new pop star in my life. 'How are you?'

'I'm great, I was just listening to Nancy and Lee and thinking of you ...'

It sounded like he was settling in for a bit of a long, leisurely, casual chat, which I definitely didn't think I was going to be able to get away with under the circumstances, even though I couldn't think of anything I would rather do.

'Listen, are you going to be around later?' I asked. 'Could I ring you back?'

'It's later I was wondering about,' he said. 'Would you like to come round for supper?'

Now I had to think quickly. 'Sure,' I said lightly. 'Can I ring you in a couple of hours and we'll chat about it?'

'That would be great.'

'OK.' I hung up quickly before he could say anything else.

'Who was that?' Pete asked sleepily, pulling me back under the duvet.

My brain racing, I remembered that Luke was listed on the phone and Pete would be able to catch me out if I lied. 'I'm doing this singing programme with a guy called Luke Lewis. He wanted to talk about the song we've been given.'

Not exactly a lie.

'I know that name, don't I?' Pete murmured, sliding his hands back down my body.

'Used to be lead singer with the West End Boys.'

'Yeah, I remember them. He was cool. Nice singing voice. You singing with him?'

'Yeah.'

'That will be cool, man.'

To stop him thinking any further I gave him a blow-job to finish him off, which sent him off to sleep like the rest of his flatmates, and I was able to slip back out on to the street a couple of hours later without any of them even opening their eyes. I dialled Luke's number as soon as I was safely in the back of a taxi.

'Hi, sorry about that, I was with some friends and it was a bit awkward …'

He gave me his address, somewhere in Fulham, and I said

I'd pop over later. I hope I sounded casual, not like my tongue was hanging out. At eight o'clock I was there, all bathed and shaved, fake-tanned and ready for action. If I'm honest, the flat was a bit of a disappointment – pretty shabby and rundown – but then I had got used to living with brand-new footballers'-wives-type stuff, so probably my taste had got a bit distorted. He looked so gorgeous I had to hold on very tightly to my self-control not to throw myself all over him the moment he opened the door, and he'd cooked me a meal. I loved Pete to death, but he'd never even shared a KitKat with me, let alone cooked me a meal. If we ever went out for a takeaway, he was always having to borrow the money off me to pay. This was the whole romantic deal: table laid up, wine chilling in the fridge, Nancy and Lee on the music system.

'I'm so pleased you came,' he said as he took my coat and hung it up. 'I've been thinking about you a lot.'

He'd been thinking about me? I'd hardly thought of anything else but him from the moment we parted at the studio a couple of days before. I'd only really gone round to Pete's to take my mind off Luke Lewis. Now I feel guilty for even saying that. I was being such a cow to Pete, but even he had to admit that Luke was 'cool'. Pete didn't rate that many people, especially singers, and certainly not singers with boy bands.

It was the best evening of my life. We'd both switched our phones off and we talked and talked – mostly about music, although I think I may have told him things about my childhood that I had never told anyone before. He was so easy to talk to. He seemed so interested in everything about me. We drank almost a bottle of wine each and did some coke and when we slid into bed together at the end of the evening it seemed like the moment I'd been waiting for ever since I was given their first album on my twelfth birthday. I'd fantasised about it so often it should have been an anticlimax, but it wasn't.

For the first time ever I turned up late for work the next day, in a taxi, straight from his place, not having learned my lines. Dora had drummed it into me a thousand times that it was the worst sin possible to be late, even for a wardrobe fitting, because one late actor could hold up a whole day's shooting and cost the production company thousands. That day, thank God, no one seemed to be too bothered because I was able to catch up on the lines in time for the first take, but it shocked me. I felt like I'd lost a little bit of control of things. It was an exciting feeling, but scary at the same time.

I couldn't stop thinking about him all day – and feeling really guilty about Pete. I decided that at the end of filming I would go round to the squat and I would tell Pete that it was time for both of us to move on. I really wanted to keep him as a friend, and I was paranoid that he would think I was dumping him because now I was the big TV star and my old friends weren't good enough for me any more. I wanted to think that I would still be able to go round on Sunday afternoons and chill out; I just didn't think the relationship was going anywhere. It was actually his mother I was most sorry about disappointing. She'd always been so sweet to me, telling me I was the only decent thing in her son's life. I don't want to sound up myself, but if I was her I would have thought the same. Pete seemed to have given up any ambition he might ever have had for his music. Doing a bit of dealing, just to give him some pocket money, seemed to be all he cared about, apart from getting high and shagging. I mean, I'm all for getting high and shagging, obviously, but it can't be your main goal in life, can it?

I had every intention of going straight there and doing the decent thing, but then Luke turned up at the studio with armfuls of flowers and whisked me off to dinner at some fancy Mayfair restaurant where the toilets were shaped like eggs and God alone knows what else.

'You didn't have to bring me to a place like this,' I said when I saw the size of the bill. 'I would have been just as happy with a pizza somewhere.'

'Pizza?' He looked puzzled, as if I'd suggested we ate his loafers. 'I like it here because people don't keep bothering you for pictures and autographs. Not that I mind doing all that stuff, but I wanted to have you all to myself.'

I know those sorts of lines are corny, but they get me every time. He'd started to open up a bit about his career and why he had agreed to take part in the singing contest.

'The problem was, we didn't write our own material,' he explained. 'We might have been selling millions of records, but we didn't own anything. They were flying us around the world, hiring limousines and private planes and hotel suites for God knows how many people, and that all had to come out of our money in the end – not to mention the costs of making the videos. I mean, we did make some money, don't get me wrong, but nothing like as much as anyone would have thought from looking at our lifestyles during those years. Now I'm pretty much living off what I can earn for gigs like this competition.'

'It's still more than most people,' I said, wanting to cheer him up because he looked so sad.

'I know, and the whole thing has been a gas, so I wouldn't change any of it. It's just that it feels like the best is behind me already. At least, it did till I met you.'

There he went again, making me feel like I was the most special person in the whole fancy room. I should have given more thought to Pete. I should have rung him and arranged to go round the next day and explain the situation. I should have done so many things, but I didn't.

I was determined not to be late to work again the next day, and I just made it, by the skin of my teeth, but I fell fast asleep in the canteen with my head on my arms over lunch. Some bright spark took my picture with their phone and the next morning I was all over the front of the tabloids, looking like some down-and-out, with the journalists all worrying about whether I was 'burning out' and asking if I was exhausted because of my eating disorder. I wanted to scream, 'I don't have a fucking eating disorder! Why do you all keep going on about it?' In the end I made some feeble joke about 'power-napping' to a journalist who managed to get my mobile number, but I don't think she was remotely convinced. Mum was round the next evening, just when I was about to pop over and see Pete, and was making cocoa and coaxing me to eat another piece of her sweet-potato pie. She's lovely, but you really can have enough of sweet-potato pie.

When Luke and I went into the studio to actually lay down the 'Summer Wine' track, there seemed to be a lot more people than usual lurking around behind the glass. I didn't have much experience of that sort of thing, but I didn't think that the men in suits were usually that much in evidence at the actual recording. Everyone was being so nice and congratulating us, it felt like we'd just got married.

'They think they've got a Christmas number one in the bag,' Luke whispered.

'Really? Shit.'

It was only later that night as I lay in bed, unable to sleep properly, that I took in the full meaning of his words. A Christmas number one? That would be so cool. I was sure Dad would like that and maybe it would make him think about letting me come home now and then. Having Christmas dinner at home would be great, especially if I could persuade Luke to come too. My sisters would think I was the coolest person on the planet if I could turn up with him. I always loved Christmas. When it came to decorating the house and wrapping all the presents it was always Mum and me who went mad. The others enjoyed it, of course they did, but they didn't go as potty with the tinsel and fairy lights as Mum and me.

Thinking of Luke made my conscience prickle and I promised myself that I would pop round and see Pete the next day and sort things out, although I wasn't sure when I would fit it in.

The actual recording of the singing competition, which they'd decided to call *Singing for their Fame*, was recorded in front of a live studio audience. They were mostly friends and relatives of the participants or fan-club die-hards. An awful lot of them seemed to need sticks and zimmer frames to get to their seats. Mum brought the girls along and they really seemed to be getting into it. They all had to do exactly what the studio staff told them, standing up and cheering and waving banners in support of their favourites – well, in support of everyone, actually – and they had to boo whenever one of the judges said anything remotely derogatory, even if it was perfectly reasonable and constructive criticism. You know the sort of thing. Mum looked really nervous whenever the camera came near her. I suppose she was afraid Dad would spot them there, although he never watched shows like that, and wouldn't watch me on principle anyway, so they were pretty safe. The girls had a really good time, which made me feel good. I so wanted them to be able to be proud of me. I was scared about what sort of things Dad might be saying about me to them. When I asked they said he never mentioned me at all, that it was like I had died, which made me feel bad in a different way.

Everyone in the audience was being so hyper and over-the-top, cheering everything and everyone, it was impossible to tell which songs or acts they'd really enjoyed the most. I knew we'd sung it well and I knew the audience had seemed to respond to the song, but I had no idea if the public would like it more or less than some of the other entries. Luke was even more nervous than I was. I suppose in a way he had more riding on it than I did. Once the competition was over I would be going back to work on

The Towers, but he would have to hustle himself up another job. I mean, I wasn't going to start feeling sorry for him or anything, I could just see it was really important to him. I could tell from how tightly he was squeezing my hand as we waited to hear the public's verdict.

They told us later, privately, that they hadn't announced the actual percentages of votes that had come in because it would have made the whole competition look pointless. Our song, apparently, swept the board. Close to a million people voted for it. A million fucking people bothered to pick up their phones and dial in, spending their money on having an opinion about a bloody song. People are amazing, aren't they? I mean, fucking hell! What must it feel like to be voted in as prime minister of a whole country or something?

Chapter Seven

'You treacherous little bitch. You're no fucking daughter of mine and never will be again.'

The call from Dad had woken me up and so it was a good few seconds after he'd hung up before I actually worked out the full impact of what he'd said. I tried ringing his number back, but he'd switched the phone off. It was the first time I'd heard his voice since leaving home and it brought back a million bad memories.

I wondered if he was angry because there'd been coverage of me and Luke in some of the papers over the previous few days. I'd been praying no one would point the stories out to Pete before I'd had a chance to go round and explain things to him. I couldn't really see why Dad should be so upset about that, though. I mean, I knew he'd liked Pete well enough, but not that well. Why would he care if I was going out with Luke? Luke wasn't married or anything, was he?

It was Sunday morning, my one chance of a lie-in that week, and I attempted to get back to sleep, but my mind was too churned up by then. I slipped out of bed, trying not to wake Luke, and went to the kitchen to make myself a cup of tea. The phone went again, this time from Dora.

'I am so sorry, darling,' were her opening words.

'Sorry about what?'

'I had no idea she was going to do that. She's out of my classes for good, I can tell you, the talentless little cow.'

'I don't know what you're talking about, Dora.' I was beginning to feel panicked now, like I was stuck in a dream where nothing anyone said to me made any sense.

'You haven't seen the papers?'

'Of course not, you know I don't read them if I don't have to.'

'That Tanya girl, the one who used to come to the same classes as you, she's sold a story about you to the *News of the World*.'

A horrible coldness ran through me as I thought back to Dad's call. Every Sunday morning his ritual was the same. Mum made him a cup of tea and then went down to the shop on the precinct to buy him a packet of fags and a *News of the World* to go with his breakfast. She was never allowed to read it until after he'd finished, so there was no chance she would have been able to censor anything she didn't want him to see.

'What kind of story?' I asked, lighting a cigarette and dragging on it deeply.

'That monologue you did the night Audrey and Tom were there, about your mum and dad. She's sold that as a story.'

'Fuck! How does she know I didn't make it up?'

'Apparently she's going out with a boy who lives on the same estate as your family. He confirmed that everyone around there knows your dad beats up your mum.'

'The newspaper just took their word for it?'

'No. They sent reporters down there knocking on doors. Everyone confirmed it.'

'Jesus. You make him sound like some kind of monster. He isn't that bad, he just can't handle his drink.'

'The press don't like wife-beaters, even if they only do it once.'

'They went to all that trouble just to write a story about Dad thumping Mum when he's had a few?' I was having real trouble getting my head around it.

'Not only that. They've splashed it across the front page. Do you want to come round here? They're all going to be on your doorstep within an hour or two, looking for a follow-up.'

If it was across the front page Mum probably had seen it first, and must have known that she had no option but to give him the paper because if he didn't get it he would know there was something wrong and would create a real stink. That must have been a truly scary moment for her, and bloody humiliating to know everyone would be talking about it.

'It's OK,' I said. 'I'm at Luke's; they don't know where I am.'

'I'm surprised none of them phoned you last night.'

'I switched my phone off until about one in the morning.'

I checked my missed calls the moment I hung up on her and sure enough there were dozens of them, none of them from numbers I recognised. How come these bastards always seemed to be able to find my number when they wanted it? By the time Luke woke up and came looking for me I'd been crying for an hour solid. Him sitting down and putting his arm around me just set me off again. I don't think I've ever cried so much for so long, shaking with sobs. It was fucking exhausting. There were so many reasons, but mainly I felt so bad for having hurt Mum and Dad like that. What happened between them was their own business. I might not always like it, but it was nothing to do with me if that was what their relationship was like. I couldn't blame Tanya for talking to the papers; she'd only done the same thing I had when I used them as raw material for my monologue. I should never have talked about private family matters in front of strangers. I'd used my mum and dad to entertain a crowd, to show off my acting skills. Dad was right, it was unforgivable and there was no way now I could undo the damage I'd done. Now everyone on the estate would be looking at them in a different way. It didn't matter that most of the men in most of the families we knew were just as handy with their fists as Dad was, some of them much worse. What mattered was that they'd been shown up in public by their daughter, one of the people who should have been protecting their privacy at all costs. Betraying your family was a far worse sin than throwing a few punches.

'What about your mum?' Luke asked. 'How will she feel?'

'She'll be gutted,' I sobbed. 'She will be so embarrassed.'

'OK.' He held me tight as he talked. 'First thing, you need to send her a quick text, saying you're so sorry and asking her to ring you.'

'What if she doesn't ring?'

'We'll cross that bridge when we get to it. I'm going to go out and get the papers so we know exactly the extent of the damage. Will you be all right for a few minutes?'

'I'm not going to top myself or anything, if that's what you mean.' I managed a feeble smile and he kissed the top of my head as he got up.

'Very pleased to hear it.'

By the time he came back with his arms full of newspapers, I hadn't moved an inch, although I had sent the text to Mum like he suggested. He laid them out on the table, made a pot of coffee and started reading. After a few minutes I mustered my courage and came to sit next to him. He gave me a grin of encouragement and passed over a *Sunday Mirror*. The front page carried a picture of him and me in a clinch at a club. It was a nice picture and a nice story, talking about how we'd fallen for each other on the programme.

'Not all bad news, you see,' he said and I nodded, still not feeling strong enough to read the *News of the World* story.

I thumbed my way half-heartedly through the other papers, finding pictures of Luke and me together in virtually all of them. It was like we were the nation's sweethearts, everyone happy for us that we'd found each other. I could almost hear 'Summer Wine' playing sickly sweet in the background to our terrifyingly public romance.

'It's not that bad,' Luke said eventually, having finished reading the whole exclusive. 'It really isn't. They're really sympathetic to you and your mum. It's going to make the public love you even more. Everyone loves someone who's had troubles in the past and has overcome them.'

'This isn't some fucking country and western song,' I snapped. 'This is my mum and dad's life.'

'I know, I know.'

Over the following few hours Luke did a brilliant job of calming me, although there was nothing he could do to raise my spirits. I still felt sick to my stomach at what I'd done, but he showed me that it didn't have to be the end of the world. 'Today's news is lining tomorrow's guinea pig cages' and all that.

One or two journalists tried to get through on the mobile, but I didn't answer any numbers I didn't recognise. Usually I tried to be polite to them when they managed to get me, but it still pissed me off. They were always so fucking charming, like they were my best friends, and then they would print complete crap, making up things that I knew perfectly well I'd never said. That was the worst thing about the *News of the World* piece: every word of it was true. It was like Tanya had been running a tape recorder that evening at Dora's. How could she remember everything I said so accurately? It was spooky, a bit like the way I was able to remember the lines from favourite movies and programmes.

Mum's call came through at about three in the afternoon. Hearing her voice made me want to cry again. 'You all right, honey?' she asked.

'I'm so sorry, Mum.'

'I know, baby. Have you had any lunch?'

'Luke's made me some breakfast. I'm not that hungry.'

'Listen, honey, I've made a pie. I'll bring some over for you this evening, about seven. You make sure you're there.'

'OK, Mum.'

'She's bringing over pie,' I told Luke as I hung up.

'There you go,' he grinned, 'so how bad can that be?'

I laughed. 'I guess.'

I was determined to be home in time for Mum's visit and I didn't want Luke to be there. This wasn't the moment that I wanted to introduce them. I wanted to have Mum all to myself for a few hours. I just wanted to cuddle into her and feel her arms round me and maybe do a bit more crying. I wanted to be her baby again, so she would forgive me. It was already dark by six o'clock when the minicab dropped me off outside my front door and I looked anxiously around for reporters. There didn't seem to be any. I had my front-door key ready in my hand to make a quick dash in. There was a streetlight just outside, which sort of illuminated the front garden like a little stage. Well, when I say 'front garden' I mean a few square feet of paving stones, which was where I left my dustbins for collection. There was one shrub, which had got a bit overgrown, but that was the only garden-type thing about the area really. Pete must have been sitting on the wall behind the bush and the bin, waiting for me. I didn't recognise him for a second and he gave me a fright, appearing out of nowhere as the cab drove off. He was wearing a hood and a thick padded jacket, but he was still shivering from the cold, or maybe it was from nerves, or possibly a bad comedown.

Thinking for a second I was being mugged, I screamed, which made him jump too.

'Jeez, Pete, you scared me.'

I felt another lurch of nausea in my stomach. I'd been telling myself I would go round to see him and break up with him properly for so long that I'd almost got used to the feeling of guilt that lurked constantly at the back of my mind. The whole thing with Mum and Dad had pushed him right out of my mind over the previous few hours, but now the guilt came rushing back.

'You fucking whore!' he spat, and that was when I saw the gun in his hand.

His eyes looked wild and a bit frightened. It seemed strange to see someone I'd known for so long and so intimately, playing such a weird, grown-up role, like a character in a movie. He was such a great guy, always so cool at school, always making me laugh in class, always performing and joking for the crowd. Everyone had envied me when I first started going out with him; it was a bit like going out with a local hero. Everyone had expected him to become some big recording star.

'You're all over the fucking papers with him.'

'I'm sorry, man, I meant to come and tell you.' I was surprised by how calm my voice sounded, like I was some sort of counsellor, talking him down off a roof somewhere. 'Please put the gun away.'

'You've made me look like a dick, man.'

I could hear footsteps behind me but I didn't dare take my eyes off Pete. There was a flash of light, and then another as Pete raised the gun. A fucking photographer? Where the fuck did he come from? Pete let off a couple of shots and I dived for cover behind the little wall separating the pavement from the garden, the explosions ringing in my ears. Everything was confusing. I saw more flashes coming from the man's camera and was aware that Pete was shouting obscenities at him. Then he was running away. My shoulder was hurting from where

I'd hit the paving and as I looked up I saw there was someone standing at a bedroom window on the other side of the street, holding up a video camera. Jesus Christ! Give me a break!

The photographer didn't bother to pursue Pete, turning his attention to me as I struggled to get up off the pavement, firing off shot after shot as I tried to work out what had happened and what I should do. He didn't offer help and I didn't ask him for any; there didn't seem any point – he had to get his pictures, he had to do his job. I knew enough by then to know what the score was going to be.

In the fall I'd dropped my front-door key and I had to scrabble around on my hands and knees trying to find it as the camera kept whirring and flashing at me from different angles. It seemed like an age before I found it, managed to pull myself to my feet and lurch towards the door. The man with the video was still standing at his bedroom window, but no one else seemed to have been attracted by the shots or the flashing of the camera. I struggled to get the door open and fell through it, slamming it behind me before I slid to the floor, panting for breath, too shocked even to cry.

Chapter Eight

Over the next few hours, things went from bad to fucking disastrous. I was just sitting on the floor in the hallway, unable to pull myself together enough to even phone Luke. I'd got the phone out but my hands were shaking uncontrollably and I couldn't trust myself not to cry if I got through to him. It wasn't so much Pete who had got to me, as the photographer. I mean, I could understand why Pete should be mad with me; I was quite surprised it hadn't happened before, but then he always had been a bit slow to pick up on what was going on around him. I hadn't realised he'd got a gun, but I wasn't that surprised about that either, given some of the people he did business with sometimes. But how could anyone have behaved like that photographer? How could you just keep taking photographs of someone who's lying on the pavement and not say anything? Not even offer to help? I mean, I know he had to have his pictures – fair enough, it's how the man earns his living. But, once he had them in the bag, couldn't he at least have helped me up and asked if I needed a cup of tea or something? I mean, it's not every day someone's ex-boyfriend pulls a gun on them in the street. I suppose not having any heart is how they are able to take pictures in war zones or in places where everyone is starving. Maybe that's the only way you can stay sane when you are faced with mountains of dead bodies and starving babies. Maybe a fallen television celebrity comes into the same category of 'man-made disaster' as far as they're concerned.

If I was shocked by what had happened outside the house, I was even more shocked when my phone started to ring. I didn't recognise the first number and answered it with a trembling thumb. Didn't recognise the voice either, a woman's voice, all cooing and sympathetic, asking if I was OK, did I need help, was I hurt? Question after question.

'Who are you?' I asked, my voice croaky.

She was only a bloody reporter, wasn't she? How the hell had she managed to get to me so quickly? I don't know if she'd talked to the photographer or the person with the video camera or what, but she seemed to know everything that had happened. I always try to be polite to reporters when they ask their really dumb questions – I mean, they've got to earn their livings too, haven't they? But I just couldn't muster the strength to do the usual bright, cheeky, cockney sparrow act. Unable to think of anything to say and not wanting her to hear me crying, I hung up. The phone rang again immediately; another number I didn't recognise. The calls kept coming and I kept cancelling them, checking each number first in case it was Mum or Luke.

When the doorbell went I nearly leaped out of my skin. I stood up, my legs wobbling under me, and peered through the peephole. I didn't recognise the face on the other side, so I just leaned back against the wall again and waited. The doorbell kept going because they knew I was in there and the phone kept ringing. So many bells jangling my nerves, making me want to scream. I could hear voices as more of them arrived, then there was some shouting, like someone was getting angry and I recognised Mum's voice. I put my eye back to the peephole. It was hard to work out what was going on in the darkness. There seemed to be a crowd and then Mum's face was the one in focus and she was calling out to me.

'Open the door, baby. Open the door, it's me!'

The moment I opened it the flashes went off again and they all started shouting their questions as Mum elbowed her way in and slammed it shut behind her.

'What the hell is going on there, girl?' she asked and I couldn't hold the tears in any longer, just sobbing and sobbing, clinging on to her as she rocked me back and forth like she used to when I came home from school to tell her I was being bullied or someone had stolen my favourite toy, just holding me tight, swaying and murmuring soothing words.

After a few minutes her magic worked and I was able to let her go. She held my hand tightly, picking up her frayed, tartan plastic shopping basket with her other hand. 'Let's warm this pie up and put the kettle on,' she said, leading me through to the kitchen.

I put the phone on silent, but I still couldn't stop myself glancing at the screen every time it vibrated. By the time Luke's number popped up I felt steady enough to talk to him.

'Hi,' his voice sounded agitated. 'What's going on? There are press all round the front door and they're all asking about you and a shooting or something. Are you OK?'

'I'm fine,' I said, just managing to stop the tears from

erupting again. 'Mum's here. Can you come over and get us? We can't stay here, the place is surrounded.'

'Sure. I'll be there as soon as I can. I'll come to the back. Are there any of them there or are they all at the front?'

'I don't know. I haven't dared open the curtains because of the cameras.'

'OK, just wait there. I'll call you when I get there.'

Half an hour later he rang again. 'I'm just parking up. The coast seems to be clear round this side. Is the garden gate unlocked?'

'I'll do it,' I said and hung up.

'You stay where you are, girl,' Mum instructed when she saw me heading for the patio door. 'I'll let him in.'

She bustled past me and I listened for the sound of voices or cameras but there was nothing. As Luke came running in with Mum puffing behind he looked so worried and I loved him for that. He gave me a big hug while Mum quickly locked the door behind them.

'What the fuck happened? The press are going mad!'

'Pete, the guy I used to date, he turned up with a gun and started firing it off, and there was a photographer and someone videoing ...'

'Jesus. Did you call the police?'

'No, I don't want the police.'

'But he's got a gun.'

'Pete's OK, he just fired it into the air. He's made his point; he won't be back. I should have told him weeks ago. It's my fault. I messed him about. I don't want to get him in trouble with the police.'

Luke opened his mouth to argue, then thought better of it. Mum had stood back respectfully to let us talk. I introduced them and Luke shook her hand and I swear to God she almost curtsied. What was that about? Sometimes I wonder about that woman.

'So we need to get you out of here,' he said, taking charge of the situation like it was some sort of SAS operation. 'Where can we drop you, Mrs McBride?'

'Joyce, you call me Joyce,' she giggled. 'Don't worry about me, I'll be fine here, you two get going.'

'Don't be stupid, Mum, we're not leaving you here,' I argued. 'You're coming with us.'

'Oh, just take me to a tube station somewhere, that will be fine.'

It wasn't worth arguing with her when she was in one of her 'humble little me' moods.

'Where are you parked?' I asked.

'Just outside. We need to go quickly before they work out there's a back door.'

Leaving all the lights on, only pausing to lock the patio door as we went, we ran down the garden and out into the deserted street behind. Luke's Range Rover was waiting, gleaming under a streetlight. As we hurried towards it I heard a camera going off and a few seconds later there were flashes and shouts and the sounds of running feet. We'd been spotted and the hunt was back on.

Luke opened the doors with a remote key and we dived in, Mum panting for breath as she hauled herself up on to the backseat. Luke already had the engine running and the car was jumping forward before she had even got her door shut and just as two cars came screaming round the corner in pursuit, flanked by what looked like half a dozen motorbikes and scooters, all carrying photographers and film cameras.

'Do your belt up,' Luke shouted and I felt the sort of fear I imagine you get in aeroplanes when the captain tells you to fasten your seatbelt.

I was scared shitless, but I have to say it was a bit of a turn-on watching Luke throwing the car round corners at God alone knows what speeds. It was a side of him I'd never seen before, taking command of the situation, and I really liked it. I mean, I'm a pretty stroppy tart most of the time, but sometimes it's nice to feel that someone else is just taking care of things for you. I can't believe I've just written that, but it's true.

Mum was alternating between muttering prayers and shaking her fists at the bikes and scooters whenever they managed to get close to the windows, their passengers firing off pictures. The cars were stuck well behind and Luke was soon able to lose them. I can't believe that any of the photographers had a clue what the story was they were following up, they must just have been told there had been an incident involving celebrities and guns and that was enough to get them pulling on their crash hats.

Must be an exciting life being a paparazzo, I suppose, a bit like fox hunting or rat catching or something. They always look like they're having a pretty good time of it, but then I suppose I don't see all the hours they put in waiting around in the rain for something to happen. They always look happy when they see me because they know it's likely to be an earner for them.

God knows how we didn't get pulled over by the police, which would have given them another lovely photo-opportunity, because Luke went mad: the wrong way up a one-way street, skidding round corners on what felt like two wheels, the whole Starsky and Hutch thing. It was probably only five minutes before he had managed to shake them all off, but it felt like a fucking lifetime.

'You all right, Mum?' I asked when he finally slowed down to a normal speed and I was able to let go of the straps and turn round.

'A little shaken up, maybe,' she grinned cheerfully and I felt so proud of her for her sweet, accepting nature.

'Sorry about that, Joyce,' Luke said. 'I think I should take Steff somewhere safe for a bit, while we work out what's going on. Do you want to come too? There'll be plenty of room and you're more than welcome.'

'Noooo,' she said – sounding a bit regretful, I thought. 'I need to get back home. He doesn't like me to not be there when he gets back at night. Just drop me at a tube station.'

She wouldn't be talked out of it and I felt horribly sad watching her walking away into the tube, still clutching her shopping bag, giving us a wave as she went. I felt like I was abandoning her in some way – stupid, I know, but that's what it felt like.

'So, where are we going?' I asked, with a bit of a forced cheerfulness, as we drove off.

'I thought we should get out of London, hide away in the

95

country for a few days,' he said. 'We'll go to my parents, there's plenty of room there.'

His parents? Fuck. I wasn't ready for that.

'We can't just turn up,' I protested.

'No, really, it'll be fine,' he assured me, squeezing my hand.

'I haven't got a sponge bag or anything.'

'They do have shops in the country,' he laughed.

I was going to have to take his word for that. I'd never actually been there myself. I'd seen it on telly and there never seemed to be many shops in sight, just moorlands or mountains or whatever, just flocks of sheep and winding little roads without pavements. I wasn't at all sure this was a good idea. If I hadn't been so completely in love with Luke by then I don't know that I would have agreed to being whisked away into the dark like that, not knowing what was waiting at our destination.

Chapter Nine

I have absolutely no idea which direction we travelled in, or how long we drove for. It started with the suburbs turning into motorways and that was when I nodded off. I remember us stopping at some service station for petrol and a pee. I tried to rush in and out quickly, so as not to be recognised, but actually there was hardly anyone there and none of them was bothering to look at anyone else, everyone concentrating on their own business in the middle of the night, all of them probably wishing they were safe in bed at home.

The next time I woke up we weren't on floodlit motorways any more and everything was dark apart from the slice of light created by our headlights, which just showed hedges and trees and the odd fox shooting across in front of us. I felt secure in the warm, leathery interior of the car and didn't want the journey to end, didn't want to have to face anyone or anything new.

When Luke put the car radio on they were playing our version of 'Summer Wine', which made us both laugh. It seemed like our voices were singing to us from another world.

I was awake when we turned into the gates of Luke's house, although I didn't realise that was what they were. They looked big enough to be an entrance to a park or something. It was only as we crunched to a stop on the gravel outside the house that I realised we had arrived. All I can say is: 'Fucking hell'. The house looked more like a hotel or maybe a local town hall. I felt like we were walking through the doors of Beckingham Palace as we came into the front hall, although I doubt if Posh lets the cobwebs build up around the chandeliers quite like they had here. There were lights blazing everywhere and the place was really warm. A giant Christmas tree was standing in the hallway, waiting to be decorated. It was the sort of size you usually only see in shopping malls. I could hear voices in the distance and laughter.

'Come on,' Luke said, taking my hand, 'let's see if we can find something to eat.'

We went past loads of doors, down a corridor that smelled a bit musty and then into a kitchen that was like some baronial hall. I half expected to see Henry VIII sitting at the end of the table, chucking chicken bones over his shoulder. There were people all round the table, which was strewn with the remains of a meal and half-empty glasses of wine. A pack of muddy-looking dogs emerged from baskets around the room, and under the table, their tails wagging as they clattered across the old tiled floor to greet Luke and sniff me out.

'Hello, darling,' a woman with grey hair and a posh accent boomed over everyone, 'what a lovely surprise.'

'Hello, Mums,' Luke said, pecking her on the cheek and waving at everyone else, 'thought we'd pop down to see you.'

'Lovely. Have you eaten? There's some lasagne on top of the oven and plenty of salad stuff in the fridge.'

'Thanks. This is Steffi, by the way.'

They all shouted out some sort of greeting. It was very friendly and it took me a few seconds to realise why it was strange. It was obvious none of them had the slightest idea who I was. That sounds really up myself, I know, but by then I had grown so used to walking into a room and knowing that everyone in there knew who I was, even though I didn't know anything about them, that I suddenly felt I'd been robbed of my identity. All this family saw was their son bringing home a new girlfriend. It was a weird feeling, a bit liberating in a way, but unnerving. I was going to have to make conversation with strangers in a way I hadn't had to for months.

The other funny thing was there was no telly on. There was a pile of Sunday papers on the side, which had obviously been well read, but none of them was the sort of paper that I was used to reading or appearing in. It was like I'd walked through another looking glass into another new world where nothing was the same as either of the worlds I was used to. In our house there was always a telly on in the background, and there were always a load of tabloid papers and magazines lying about the place. If an actress from any of the soap operas had walked through the door unexpectedly, it would have been like a Martian had landed, or a member of the Royal Family.

Luke sat me down while he loaded me up a plate of food from the top of their cooker, which was one of those giant old things that stay hot all the time, with loads of doors and big silver lids to be lifted off the top to get at the hot plates. Everyone was talking at once, making sure I had a glass of wine and a napkin and cutlery, while continuing the conversations they must have been having when we walked in. I stayed quiet and ate, suddenly realising how hungry I was. Luke sat next to me, protecting me from having to make conversation for a while as I tried to work out who everyone was.

His mum was the loudest one in the party, very strong and in control of everything. His dad was still picking at bits of the paper at the same time as coming in and out of conversations, his glasses perched on the end of his nose, his grey hair sticking out all over the place from where he kept running his fingers through it, looking puzzled. He had a lot of stains down the front of his jumper and his elbows were poking through holes in the sleeves. There were a couple of young men who looked similar to Luke, and I gradually learned they were his brothers. One of them had a woman sitting beside him who was nursing a small baby as she talked; another young woman was busily making hot drinks for everyone. There was an elderly lady, who seemed to be Luke's grandmother. I guessed she was his mother's mother as she had the same sort of loud, commanding voice.

The dogs were milling around underneath me, and one rested its chin on my lap, which looked quite sweet and made me feel very at home, even though it smelled a bit rank and left a patch of dribble behind it.

'Where's Grandpa?' Luke asked.

'He's just dashed back upstairs,' his mother replied. 'Some programme he had to watch.'

As soon as I'd finished eating, Luke swept me up again.

'Let's go and find Grandpa,' he said, ushering me from the room before I could even say thank you for the food.

'Your family are awesome,' I said as he led me by the hand up a small back staircase.

'Thanks. My grandfather is a bit of a silver surfer, and I thought it might be worth having a look on the Internet to see if there is anything about you. He has satellite TV as well.'

Luke's grandfather didn't look much older than his parents, and seemed particularly happy to see his grandson. It looked to me like the two of them had some kind of special bond. His room was part bedroom and part office, with paper everywhere.

'This is Steffi, Grandpa,' Luke said.

'Very pretty too,' the old man said.

'Thanks.' I felt much more comfortable now.

'Want a drink, either of you?'

'Cheers, Grandpa.'

Luke went over to a tray of bottles and glasses and poured us each a shot of whisky. 'Mind if I have a quick look on the Internet, Grandpa?' he asked, coming back with my glass.

'Of course – what are you looking for?'

'Steff had a spot of bother with the media before we left London, just wondered if it was being reported.'

'Oh, right.' He didn't seem remotely surprised by the information. 'Want me to have a look at the news channels?'

'That would be great,' Luke replied, indicating for me to sit down on an old sofa in the corner of the room, where an ancient-looking terrier growled at me ominously without bothering to raise its head.

'Take no notice,' the old man said. 'It's all bluff; he's got no teeth.'

As they both worked the keyboard and television control,

it felt like watching two overgrown schoolboys; Luke even stuck his tongue out in concentration as he worked. It wasn't long before they had found what they wanted. We were all over the news. The film that my kindly neighbour had been shooting from the window opposite was everywhere. It was grainy and impossible to make out Pete's face, but you could see the gun and hear the shots. The photographer had also managed to get his pictures distributed and there were some bloody unflattering shots of me lying on the pavement. The stories all ended with more shots of Luke's Range Rover roaring away and the voice-overs all talked about me 'going into hiding'. They didn't seem to have made the connection with Luke yet, but since you could clearly see the car's number plate, although it had been fogged out for the public, I guessed it wouldn't be long before he was dragged into it.

'You've had a busy evening, you two,' the old man said with a chuckle.

'Steff's the girl I've been doing this television singing competition with, Grandpa.'

'Ah, yes.' The old man peered at me more closely. 'I can see it now. Nice voice you have.'

'Thanks.'

'Grandpa's the only one around here who shows any interest in my career.'

'That's not true,' the old man protested. 'They're all very proud of you.'

We sat with Grandpa for an hour or more and it felt like the rest of the world had melted away outside that comfy, chaotic room, even though there were images flickering on the television and computer screens, reminding us of what was going on in the rest of the world. Eventually, Luke decided it was time for us to leave the old boy in peace.

'Tired?' he asked and I nodded. 'Come on, I'll show you my room.'

Luke's room was up another staircase and along another corridor and it didn't look as if anything had been touched in there since he was 14. His duvet even had a picture of Superman on it.

'Jesus,' I said, 'this whole place is like some museum.'

'Sorry.'

'No, don't be stupid. It's really nice. I wish I'd had a room like this.'

There was a school photo on the wall, all of them in blazers and looking like right little toffs. Luke showed me himself and the other members of the band. Seeing such familiar faces in such unfamiliar surroundings was spooky. There was another picture of them in a football team – sorry, 'rugby', like that made any difference.

'Different-shaped ball,' he laughed, pointing out the ball he was holding in the picture, which looked more like an Easter egg. 'Very different game.'

Whatever.

That night he held me tightly in his little single bed, cuddled up under Superman, and I felt safer than I'd ever felt before.

By the next morning the family had obviously got some idea from Grandpa of what was going on. They now knew I was an actress and that I was having some trouble with the media but his mum seemed to be more interested in how many pancakes we wanted for breakfast.

Dora rang just as I was tucking into my fourth and Luke's mum was dishing his fifth up on to his plate from the Aga (see how quickly I was catching on to the lingo?).

'You all right, darling?' Dora asked, not pausing for an answer. 'Where are you?'

'In the country,' I replied, not having any more detailed information than that.

'Really?' The concept seemed to puzzle her as much as it had me. 'That's nice. Have you seen the news today?'

'Nothing since last night.'

'Well, the police have tracked your Pete down to his lair and he's done a runner. The squat is empty, if you don't count the fifty or so photographers crawling around it, photographing every sordid detail.'

'Is Pete all right?'

'I have no idea, and less interest. I hope they find him and lock him up.'

'Oh, don't say that.' I felt an actual stab of pain at the thought of poor old Pete being locked up just for letting off a few shots in the street. I felt so bad about his mum. She'd worked so hard to make her family respectable and to give Pete a good start in life. This publicity would finish her and it felt like it was all my fault.

'Well, you know my views on that young man. Anyway, don't forget you have filming for the finals of *Singing* this week. Do you want me to arrange a car to pick you up from wherever you're hiding out?'

'I'll talk to Luke.'

'OK, let me know if you need anything.'

I was shocked when I saw the pictures of Pete's squat in the papers. I suppose I'd never really seen it in full daylight because we always had the windows boarded up and covered with old sheets or paintings we'd done ourselves. When we did have the lights on we usually had coloured bulbs, or put scarves over them to dull them down and make them more psychedelic. I'd brought in a set of fairy lights as well, which made the place look quite romantic, but there was no sign of them in the pictures. Mainly it was the people who had made it feel friendly and cheerful, and they had long gone by the time the photographers arrived, along with anything homely like sleeping bags or posters. I suspect the photographers might have adjusted the scene a bit themselves to make it look even bleaker and more disgusting – 'every parent's worst nightmare' and all that. It looked like we'd been living in some graffiti-strewn underpass. They didn't go quite as far as showing discarded syringes on the floor, but they might as well have because that's what the whole thing looked like.

They'd also managed to find a picture of Pete from when we were at school. He must have been posing for the camera that day, trying to look hard, because it wasn't how he normally looked, more like the kind of hard-nosed criminal that the tabloids love to frighten their readers with, just the sort who would take revenge on his girlfriend with a gun. Why would anyone think that I would have fallen for someone who seemed so cold-eyed and vicious? Maybe they liked the idea of me as victim to this satanic figure, maybe that was the fantasy they were playing to. In reality Pete was always so warm and relaxed, always laughing and teasing, when he wasn't comatose with something, but that wasn't the image the media needed. They needed a villain for their story, a bad man who had driven their hero and heroine (that's me and Luke, in case you're not getting where I'm going with this) into hiding. It was very nice of the media to be so concerned for our safety, but a bit rough to demonise poor harmless old Pete for the sake of a few shock-horror headlines. But that's the name of the game, I suppose. They like to package everything up as a series of fairy tales, populated by evil villains and innocent heroines. For a few days poor old Pete was up there in their demons' gallery with folk like Saddam Hussein and the Yorkshire Ripper.

'Jesus,' Luke said when he saw the pictures. 'Is that what he looks like?'

'No,' I tried to reassure him, 'not at all. They've just taken a bad picture of him. He's really sweet looking.'

I could tell that this was backfiring on me, making it sound like I still fancied Pete, which was only marginally better than leaving Luke feeling shit-scared that he was going to be gunned down in the street by some Yardie heavy, so I shut up.

As well as going after Pete, the photographers had also been tailing Dad to and from the pub. Although Pete was top of their list of public enemies now, Dad was still in there as the wife-beater and father from hell, and there were plenty of reporters who wanted to kick him while he was down. I could imagine exactly how they would have been taunting him, trying to provoke him into doing something violent that they could snap, illustrating the role that he had been allotted in this whole scenario. I dare say some of them had been buying him a few vodkas to help fuel the fire. He didn't disappoint them and the papers were full of pictures of him lurching around, throwing punches and ending up on the floor. This was exactly what he must have been talking about when he said he didn't want the media 'sniffing through our bins'. He'd been right and I felt terrible, but what could I have done different? Should I have stayed in the hotel kitchens, washing up for the rest of my life? That didn't mean I didn't feel guilty. I knew I could have handled Pete a bit more diplomatically, and I certainly shouldn't have done that riff in Dora's class about Dad and Mum.

How was I ever going to make it up to him? How was I ever going to be able to make my peace with him without giving up the job that I was enjoying so much? Was that really the only choice I had?

Chapter Ten

We were recording for the final of *Singing for their Fame* (and yes, since you ask, the irony in the title *was* starting to get on my tits). It was going well and everyone kept telling Luke and me we were going to win with 'Summer Wine'. We were going to be doing two songs for this show and I had asked to do one that I knew was Mum's favourite. It's called 'A Little Time' by The Beautiful South and she used to listen to it all the time when she was cooking. I'd come into the kitchen and she'd have it on with tears running down her face.

It's like a duet between a man, who's saying he needs 'a little time' and 'a little space' – like the bastards always do – and the girl singing back to him, really sharp and witty. In the end he realises he's made a mistake and wants to come back and by that time she's realised she's better off without him. Really good stuff. I love songs that tell stories like that. All the time I was hanging out with Pete listening to trance and rap and God knows what else, I was probably a closet country-and-western fan really. Not that The Beautiful South are country, of course.

'I don't know ...' Luke was doubtful when I first suggested

it. 'You know the media will think it's about us, that I've been messing you about. If they think that they'll make me public enemy number one.'

'Don't you think you're taking this a bit seriously?' I laughed. 'It's just a fucking song. Frank and Nancy Sinatra sang a love song together and they were father and daughter, for fuck's sake!' I was learning fast.

'Yeah, but you are the nation's sweetheart at the moment and the tabloids can be more protective than any shotgun-toting older brother. You've seen that from the way they've turned on Pete and your dad.'

'My God, get a grip,' I said. 'It's a funny song. It'll make them laugh while they're crying.'

'OK,' he gave in. 'You win – as always.'

I was so happy to be doing it for Mum. I knew she'd be in the audience with the girls and she would be surprised that I had remembered the song. I wanted to do something special for her. I couldn't get the image of her walking off to the tube station out of my head; she had looked so small and vulnerable. I mean, she's not small, not by any stretch, but she looked small in the crowd, so alone, while I was driving off in the big warm flash car with the man of my fantasies and she had to stagger home to a bad-tempered drunk and a load of housework.

The police turned up halfway through recording, which was pretty fucking embarrassing, and I had to go off to a side room with them. They were really keen that I should press charges against Pete, but I was adamant I wasn't going to. It was bad enough he'd been driven out of his home because of me, I wasn't going to get him landed in court. I told them I couldn't be sure it was him, that I hadn't been able to see his face in the hood. I could tell they didn't believe me and they actually started to get pretty threatening, which did not bring out my best side. The stroppier I got, the heavier they got and things were about to get very bad indeed when Luke came to the rescue yet again.

One minute they were practically threatening to arrest me and have me banged up and the next they were on their feet pretty much doffing their caps to Luke, just because he's some old pop star; or maybe because he is really good at doing that patrician thing with his voice, which makes it quite clear that he's one of them, not one of us. You wouldn't think the modern police force would still be impressed by all that old crap, would you? But he almost had them apologising for wasting his valuable time. I tell you, I'm going to get Dora to teach me to speak like that. I'll tell her it's for a part. She calls it 'RP' which apparently stands for 'received pronunciation', sort of like the Queen sounds.

The show went really well. Everyone kept saying we were the favourites to win, which made me jumpy in case people thought they didn't need to vote for us because we were a sure thing. The producers were doing everything they could to rev up the number of calls being made, building the tension and making us all really nervous and close to tears. The presenter kept asking us to appeal to the voting public and the other competitors all kept giving these really creepy little speeches about how honoured they felt to be there at all and how grateful they were to everyone. I was having real trouble getting my tongue round any of that, so I left it up to Luke and just hung on his arm, hoping I looked like I was keeping my sense of irony but probably just looking a bit arrogant.

They caught me out when I started to talk about dedicating my song to Mum and wanting to give my money to her children's home if I won. I started out talking about it quite normally, live on camera, and then my eyes watered up and my voice cracked. The camera swung on to Mum in the audience, just as I had expected, and I could see her eyes wide with surprise. In fact, she looked more shocked than moved, as if it had never occurred to her that any of us had taken any notice of the songs she listened to when she was alone and thoughtful. My tears must have looked really fake to viewers but actually they weren't, which was a surprise to me. Every time I thought about Mum I was getting a bit tearful and I wasn't sure why. It wasn't like I wasn't getting to talk to her on the phone whenever I wanted, and I could easily arrange to see her when I needed to. So why did just thinking about her make me so sad?

'Hormones, probably,' was Luke's suggestion after my little crack-up in front of the camera, which is the sort of annoying thing men say when they can't be bothered to give something any thought at all.

Despite the fact that the whole phone-in thing was really just a giant money-making scam by the production company and everyone else involved, I couldn't help feeling really moved when it was announced on the final live show that we had won. Even though I knew millions of copies of 'Summer Wine' were already in the shops waiting to be released into the Christmas market to mop up every last consumer who needed an emergency stocking filler for someone in their family, by the time the presenters had finished building the suspense I was tense as a whippet and Mum was covering her face with her hands in the audience. Then there was a long silence before the announcement and an explosion of tears as the dam burst. Mum and the girls were jumping up and down like little kids, tears streaming down their faces. Even Luke was crying. God knows how those actresses hold it together at all when they win Oscars with all the build-up that goes into that. If I ever win one of those – and don't think I haven't got my acceptance speech already down pat – I'm going to be a complete 'hormonal' puddle.

The nicest bit about the whole thing was seeing how happy Luke was to be back on top. It was only a television show, even if it was being watched by close to 10 million people, but it seemed like the whole world at that moment. I was standing with the man I had been in love with since I was 12, soaking up the adoration of the audience and God knows how many telephone voters. I think it would have been impossible not to be a bit freaked out.

★　　★　　★　　★

The whole Pete fuck-up wasn't going so well. The papers seemed to be building him up into some kind of symbol of everything that was going wrong with the great British 'underclass' – which is one of the least charming ways of describing anyone, don't you think? Everyone who had ever known him was coming out of the closet and telling stories about his drug deals, making out like he was corrupting

the entire youth of the world, when all he was was a bit of
a dopehead.

I was trying to ignore the papers as much as possible. A few
of them seemed to have been able to track me down to Luke's
family palace, but they were too intimidated to make it past
the stately gates and demented packs of off-duty gun dogs that
seemed to roam around all the time. I was just driven up to
the studios each morning, dodging whatever journalists were
waiting outside, and then driven back again at night. I heard
that there was a permanent contingent of photographers
camped outside my house, so there was no way I was going
back there yet.

I was still horribly aware of just how much of a witch hunt
was building up and eventually, after a good few glasses of
wine, I plucked up the courage to ring Pete's mum. The
moment I heard her tired, sad voice I was fighting back the
tears again. She told me none of the family had heard
anything from him since the night of the incident and that set
me right off. I was sobbing and snuffling away and saying how
sorry I was, over and over again.

'You've got nothing to be sorry about, lovey,' she said.
'You've done nothing wrong. I told him over and over that
you were the best thing that ever happened to him and that if
he didn't pull himself together he was going to lose you. He's
got no one to blame but himself.'

That did it. There's nothing like a bit of kindness to really
hit the emotional meltdown button.

'I just feel so bad for him,' I sobbed, 'and for the others in
the squat, who lost their home.'

'Don't you go wasting your sympathy on them,' she scolded. 'They all needed a kick up the rear to get them going. They couldn't stay in that terrible place forever.'

'Have you heard from any of them?'

'They've been in touch, but you're not to be taking any notice of anything any of them is saying.'

That was the first inkling I had that I maybe should be worrying about what was going on with the others from the squat.

'Why, what have they been saying?'

'Oh, you're not to worry about any of that. We don't think any of this is your fault.'

'But they do?'

'They're just jealous of your success. You take no notice, they'll come round.'

It was nice to know that she didn't hold any grudges against me, but I still came off the phone with a new lead weight in my stomach. These people had been the nearest things I had to friends all through my time at school. Even though I knew they only really tolerated me because I was with Pete, they were still the closest friends I'd had so far. We'd been through puberty together, for Christ's sake, and a fair bit more besides. I didn't like the idea that they might be bad-mouthing me around the place. Pete's mum might not be taking any notice of them, but there were always people who were keen to think the worst of anyone who appeared on telly or in the press. It sounds pathetic to say it, but I just wanted everyone to like me.

When I told Luke about my worries he suggested I ring

them and put my side of the story, show them that I wasn't putting on any airs or graces just because I'd had a bit of good luck. It sounded like good advice, but when I tried to ring their mobiles none of them picked up. Maybe that should have rung some alarm bells, but all it did was make me sad about how much of my past I had lost.

I don't know how I would have coped without Luke and his family. It just seemed to be taken for granted that I would be staying with them for Christmas. They never questioned me about my situation or anything else, just included me in all their family rituals. Despite all their efforts to make me feel a million per cent comfortable I couldn't help but feel like an outsider, finding myself thinking about Mum and the others and what they would be doing at any given moment. Luke's mum said I was welcome to invite my family over, but I knew that wouldn't work. If they had felt uncomfortable in my little house, imagine how they would have felt there.

When 'Summer Wine' sold more copies than any Christmas single since God alone knows when, the news actually seemed to filter through to Luke's family that I was a celebrity (cringe, cringe), but they still didn't seem that interested. The song came on the radio in the kitchen once or twice and Luke's mum commented on how much she liked it in a polite sort of way, but nothing else. And when the first of my old school friends' 'exclusives' appeared in the *News of the World* it didn't seem to impinge on their world at all.

I know it didn't bypass them completely because this time one or two brave journalists actually made it up to the house, or rang the house phone, but Luke's dad just told them to fuck off (using different but obviously much more effective words) and they did. I guess they have an automatic respect for people who look like they could afford the best lawyers and wouldn't hesitate to use them. Apparently, one of Luke's brothers was a red-hot media lawyer and Luke said he would be happy to help if I wanted. I said I didn't want to get into all that. The whole idea of lawyers and courts frightened me sick, if I'm going to be honest. I thought it would be better to just keep my head down and wait for the whole storm to blow over rather than risking making it worse by creating a fuss.

There were two girls in particular who had obviously cashed in big time with the paper. Apparently, they had been to see a publicist called Quentin James, who Luke told me was well known for selling these sorts of stories for really high prices.

'I'm surprised you haven't heard of him,' he said.

'Why?'

'He's infamous, a talking head on the telly, gets on the news every time there's some sort of new scandal or sleaze exposé. He's got a finger in everything; disgraced politicians, adulterous footballers, misbehaving royals, the lot. He'll probably be ringing you next, offering to tell your side of the story. Just about everyone ends up in his office eventually.'

'Fuck that.'

'He can be good for putting your side of the story across. The editors listen to him. He did some stuff for the West End Boys when we were trying to get some media attention.'

'Dad would have a fit if I started mouthing off in the

117

papers. That's exactly the sort of thing he's been on about from the start.'

'Do you think you really need to worry about what your father thinks when he won't even speak to you?'

'Fuck off,' I replied, not willing to even go there.

I suppose I'm kidding myself when I say these girls were my friends in school. Actually, they were just a couple of slags who liked to hang around Pete. In fact, they probably hated me from the start because I was the one who got off with him (not that I'm kidding myself he didn't shag them too from time to time). I was never quite part of their gang. They caught me reading books once or twice, and the fact that I hung out with Dave discussing plays in break times meant they had me down as a total geek. I guess they only really tolerated me to please Pete, now I think about it. That's a bit bloody depressing.

Most of what they wrote in the papers about our times in the squat was pretty accurate when it came down to it – it was just the way they phrased it that made it sound so bad. I guess that may have been down to the reporters they were talking to rather than them. I know all too well how they can twist your words to give a different meaning when they want to. The basic gist of their stories was that I had been a hooker – which is a bit of a showstopper as accusations go, really.

I've never for a moment thought of myself as being on the game, but there were occasions when Pete couldn't afford to pay one or other of his suppliers, and he would ask me to help out. Usually it was just a quick hand job, or a blow-job if they weren't too disgusting and if Pete owed them an awful lot, but it was never full sex. Having said that, there were a few parties where we all mixed and matched, but I had never been aware of any money changing hands. These two seemed to have different memories. All I can say is if there was money changing hands no one ever told me about it. I'm not saying I would have done anything differently if I had known, I'm just saying … I guess I'm just saying I must have been a bit more naive than I would have liked to think at the time.

I can see why it looks bad when I describe it like that, but it never seemed that big a deal to me. It certainly wasn't for Pete, who knew exactly what was going on, and was often the one who suggested it. If you love someone you don't mind doing them the odd favour, do you?

Whatever it may have seemed like to me, it was certainly a big deal to the media now. 'Steffi's vice-girl past' became the big running story in every tabloid over the next few days and the rest of the press overcame their reticence to travel to the country and set up camp outside the mighty gates of Luke's family estate, snapping and shouting at every car that drove in or out. The story fitted so nicely with the plot lines Nikki had in *The Towers*, and contrasted so beautifully with the on-screen romance Luke and I had been playing out for all to see while singing our sweet little duets, that everyone wanted to read more – or, at least, the editors believed they did.

Although his family were incredibly cool about the whole thing, just pretending it wasn't happening most of the time, I could see Luke was having a bit of trouble getting his head round some of the detail that was being gloated over by the great British reading public. It was the first time I had seen him really lost for words. He should have known what the media were like better than most; God knows the West End Boys suffered from more than their fair share of inaccurate rumours and stories in their time. But this one did seem to have got him rattled.

'Is it true?' he asked, after reading the first of the slappers' stories.

'Well, I'm not a fucking "vice girl" if that's what you mean,' I snapped, unreasonably cross with him for the wet way he was looking at me. 'But we did do some pretty wild partying.'

'So it is true?'

'We were only kids,' I protested, unable to understand why he wasn't treating the newspapers' hypocritical mock outrage as a joke like he usually did. 'We were straight out of school, just messing about. No one died, for Christ's sake.'

I was probably getting a bit tearful again and he gave me a hug, but didn't offer any words of comfort, which pissed me off.

I'm not easily embarrassed, mainly because I haven't done that much in my life that I'm ashamed of, but this was a bit of a setback. I still didn't really regret anything I'd done, but I wouldn't necessarily have wanted to share it with the whole world. I mean, taking a dump is one thing, taking a dump in the middle of Trafalgar Square on New Year's Eve quite another, if you get my drift. This is the thing about fame: there are just some things you would rather not do in front of the whole bloody world, and that includes giving blow-jobs to passing scumbags. But the worst thing was that the girls were claiming I'd betrayed Pete, sold him up the creek (a bit rich, coming from a couple who were definitely selling me up the creek). They were implying that I had turned my back on my old friends and wasn't therefore the 'nice girl next door' that I pretended to be. Well, I've never pretended to be anything – unless I was acting, that is. It was the reporters who decided to make out that I was some sort of 'tart with a heart', but now the same journalists seemed to be keen to show that I had somehow tricked them into thinking I was a loveable working-class character when actually I was some sort of ambitious, social-climbing, scheming, treacherous, 'vice girl' bitch. Well, thank you soooo much! In fact, they were making things far worse for Pete than I had, because now the press thought he was a pimp as well as a gun-toting junkie.

Once the story was out there, and once I was back in London, every reporter in the world seemed to be banging on the door or ringing me to try to get my side of events. Apparently, it's always a bit quiet for news in the New Year. They were all really sympathetic and keen to help. 'We can offer you protection,' they all said. 'We could take you to a secure location and make sure no one else bothers you. Then you could have the opportunity to tell your story in your own words.'

They all said exactly the same thing, more or less. 'What they are actually saying,' Luke explained, 'is that you should sign an exclusive contract with them and they will then make sure none of their rivals can get near you to write a spoiler.'

'I don't want to talk about it to anyone.' I was categorical.

'Then don't accept any of their offers. Retain a dignified silence.'

But that didn't stop them from asking. They were more persistent than any telephone-sales person. They were driving me fucking mad; I came so close to giving in and going with one of them, just to shut them all up, which was exactly what they were after, of course.

Usually when something went wrong in the papers, Mum would give me a ring to check I was all right. In fact, sometimes that was the way I found out that something had appeared in the first place. But this time there was a deafening silence from that direction. I could imagine just how Dad must be crowing, as if this was proving he was right to chuck me out of the house. He was probably dumping all the blame on her head for supporting me in my dreams to be an actress and not backing him up when he tried to put a stop to them.

It took me a little while to pluck up the courage to ring her after the latest set of revelations and when I did she put a brave face on it as usual, but I could tell she was shaken by the whole thing. She didn't suggest coming round to give me something to eat and a hug, but maybe she thought Luke would be handling that side of things now. It was an odd conversation, like we had become strangers. It left me feeling deeply sick, like my soul had been bruised.

I dreaded going back to work after Christmas, when I knew everyone would have read the stories. I half expected to be told that Nikki was going to have to be written out of the series, but it was like nothing had happened. The other actors were all so used to reading things about one another and themselves that they just assumed the whole thing was a fabrication and didn't even bother to comment, apart from the odd passing commiseration. The producers said nothing to me, but Dora informed me they were now even keener to sign me up for the next few months – so keen that she was holding out for more money.

'You are by far the most famous person in the series at the moment,' she explained, when I expressed my surprise. 'You're their star; they aren't going to want to lose you while you're so hot. We have to make the most of it while it lasts.'

She was turning out to be such a good businesswoman on my behalf it was hard to understand why she had never been able to make money for herself in the past. She also seemed to be totally unconcerned about the nature of the stories.

'They're all begging for interviews,' she said. 'Every paper and magazine has been on to me, and all the sofa shows.'

'I don't want to talk to anyone, in case I drop Pete even further in the crap. And I really don't want to be having hundreds of conversations about blow-jobs with leery reporters.'

'It might be good to do just one big TV interview, so you can set the record straight, put it all in perspective. We could lay some ground rules for what they can and can't ask. It helped Hugh Grant when he did *Letterman*, and *Parkinson* did wonders for George Michael when he had that trouble in the public toilet.'

'OK,' I said, 'if you think I should.'

I would really have liked Luke to come on the show with me, but he was acting a bit funny about the whole thing, so I decided not to push my luck. He kept going into long, silent moodies, and then swearing there was nothing wrong when I asked him. To be honest, it was beginning to get on my tits a bit. All I really wanted to do was concentrate on my acting, do a bit of singing if anyone asked and spend as much time as I could with him. It should all have been going so well, but somehow it just didn't feel right any more. It felt like something even worse might be brewing up on the horizon, that these stories had just been warning rumbles of thunder and the real storm was yet to come.

Chapter Eleven

Jonathan Ross – what a star the man is. It was like chatting to one of Dad's leery mates in the pub. He asked his questions with a mixture of innuendo and irony which made the whole thing seem like a storm in a teacup.

Dora had always said that a good actress can sense the mood of an audience, and I felt I could sense a strong affection in that studio. If I looked up I could see older women smiling at me indulgently, like I was their favourite cheeky granddaughter, and I swear that the men whose eyes I caught while I was signing autographs afterwards all blushed. What was that all about? Probably best not to think about it.

The papers were still ranting on about how I was an example of everything that was morally wrong with the young people today, that Pete and I and the others at the squat were typical examples of the 'disenfranchised underclass' (that bloody word again), but these people I met, who were presumably readers of all these papers, didn't seem to be judging me at all. It was all a bit confusing, especially when Mum and Luke, the two people I cared about the most, were acting all odd.

Dora had been keeping all the articles that were appearing,

good and bad, and eventually I plucked up the courage to go round to her place and go through them. She said it would be good for me to understand fully what was being said. She opened a bottle of red wine and rolled a joint and we settled down at her kitchen table with the cats wandering about over the papers as we read. She was right; when looked at with a cool head, it wasn't so bad. Quite a lot of journalists had come out saying that I hadn't done anything wrong, that my openness and honesty was very refreshing and should be applauded. Even some of the ones that had ranted the most when the accusations were first made were mellowing in the face of readers' letters and a general reluctance on the part of the public to get their knickers in a twist over anything so stupid. One article got all serious about my acting – in *The Towers*, for Christ's sake – claiming that the reason I brought such 'depth' and 'power' to the role was because I had so much emotional baggage to draw on. I rather liked that one, read it twice and highlighted 'depth' and 'power' with Dora's yellow pen thing.

'You've had a few interesting offers too,' Dora said, once I'd read all I needed to. 'I've had a call from a publisher asking if you would like to do a book.'

'Me, write a book? Do they know I didn't even get my English GCSE?'

'They'd give you a ghostwriter for that.'

'Nah, that would be the final nail as far as Dad was concerned.'

'The other offer that I think might be worth considering is a revival of *Sweet Charity* in the West End, playing Charity.'

'Seriously? The Shirley MacLaine part? I love that movie.'

'It is another hooker, of course – well, a sort of hooker – so we'd have to think about typecasting.'

'And what about *The Towers*?'

'That's the other thing we'd have to consider. The way things are going at the moment I could probably get you six months off to do the play, with Nikki coming back again later. But maybe it's time to move on anyway.'

This was a shocker. I had sort of imagined that I would be doing Nikki till they threw me off. I imagined myself hanging on like Ken Barlow in *Corrie*, or Dot Cotton in *EastEnders*. It hadn't occurred to me that it might just be a stepping stone to something bigger. I think the media always assume that someone like me has some grand career plan, but how would that work? How could I have foreseen any of the stuff that was happening to me that year?

'My God, Dora. I thought this would be it. I thought I'd be playing Nikki till I was all wig and wrinkles.'

'That's partly why the public loves you so much,' she said, topping up my glass.

'Why?'

'Because you haven't the faintest idea how good you are. It's very appealing.'

That made me feel a bit of a fraud, because I had always thought I was pretty good at the acting and singing, I just hadn't imagined that I would be able to break into the business so easily.

'You don't have to make up your mind yet, but it does put you in a strong bargaining position. They have been asking if

127

you would be interested in doing *Chicago*, too, but everyone does that. *Sweet Charity* would be better because she's such a nice character. The women in *Chicago* are such bitches.'

'Fantastic parts, though.' I couldn't believe we were actually having this conversation. I was turning down parts in West End shows because my agent didn't like the characters? How weird was that?

'And they've asked if you and Luke will present an award at the next Brits Awards ceremony.'

'That would be so cool.'

'I told them,' she continued as if I hadn't spoken, 'that you would only do it if you and Luke got to perform a song of your choice.'

My God, Dora was turning into Colonel Tom Parker before my very eyes.

'Perform at the Brits? Are you sure? If they thought Michael Jackson was a sell-out, what are they going to think of the winners of something as naff as *Singing for their Fame*? They'll boo us off the stage, won't they?'

'I don't think so. You are both very popular at the moment, and you're selling a fuck of a lot of records. Do you think Luke would be up for it?'

'I'll ask him.'

I knew bloody well he would be up for it. It was just the sort of credibility he craved, putting him right back where he was before the group split, but I thought it was only respectful to ask him first. He was just as excited as I'd expected.

'I think we should do something other than "Summer Wine",' I suggested.

'But everyone loves it,' he protested.

'I know, but they'll be bored of it soon. Let's do "A Little Time" and camp it up a bit.'

He wasn't hard to persuade and, to my amazement, nor were the record company or the Brits organisers. I couldn't get my head round the way that everyone was happy to do whatever I asked for. I didn't notice it at first, but once I had noticed it I saw it all the time. It started out being really nice, but then it began to get on my nerves a bit. I think that was why I liked being with Luke's family and Dora, because they treated me like I'd always been treated. I wasn't comfortable with being pandered to, like I was a star. I was still the same person who had been washing dirty dishes a few months before, being shouted at by a load of sweaty chefs. One of the main reasons why I wasn't comfortable about it was because I could see it was really pissing off the other cast members at *The Towers*, and I could completely understand their point of view. None of them minded me doing publicity stuff, because they all got to do that from time to time, but, when it was known that the production staff were consulting me about developments in Nikki's character, the whispers really started.

Actors on soaps look like they're getting all the glory, with their red-carpet moments and the features in magazines and all the rest, but actually they're pretty low in the pecking order at the actual television companies. Really distinguished actors can find their characters killed off without any warning and anyone protesting too often about some lines they have been given, or some piece of business, will soon find themselves called into the office and dressed down like a naughty school kid. I'd never had it happen to me because basically I'd been doing exactly what I was asked, but I knew several who did.

When things went wrong for the actors in their personal lives, the company would make all sorts of statements about us being one big family and all sticking together, but actually they were only interested in ratings. If an actor pissed off the press by two-timing his wife with a hooker, his days were numbered – which was what made it strange that no one was cross with me about the squat revelations. There seemed to be some double standards at work here. Because I was young and considered a bit sexy, I was allowed to get away with things that would have ended the careers of some of the older men. Thank God for it, of course, but it didn't make any of us feel too secure. We all wondered when the tide of public sympathy would turn against us.

'It's the public who decides our fate,' one old hand told me early on. 'If they decide they don't want to see you any more then you'll be out faster than any politician. If the powers-that-be believe you're putting bums of seats, then they'll be crawling up your arse morning, noon and night.'

They seemed to think I was putting bums on seats, which was nice to know, but I didn't like the idea that the others might think I was getting above myself.

Performing at the Brits was like a dream come true. Luke said it was like the first time the West End Boys went on *Top Of The Pops*. There were so many stars backstage I just walked around with my mouth hanging open, forcing myself not to ask for autographs. They all said 'hi' so casually it was like I was one of them, like we had known each other forever. I swear to God half of them wouldn't have known me from a hole in the ground, probably thought I was some groupie who had managed to get past security. I was given this incredible dress by Stella McCartney. Stella McCartney, for fuck's sake! It was all so weird.

'Am I doing your make-up?' one of the girls in the Make-Up department asked as I sat in her chair.

'Yeah, is that all right?'

'Of course. I just thought you'd have your own people. Most of the stars come with an entourage of stylists and make-up artists and all the rest.'

'Nah,' I replied, not sure what the correct response was. Was she suggesting I was a star? I assumed she was talking about people like Madonna, J-Lo, Gwen Stefani and the rest, not someone from the cast of *The Towers*. I wasn't sure if she was sending me up or not. As we chatted I realised she wasn't being horrible or anything, just speaking her mind. She was really nice and offered to put me in touch with all sorts of people if I needed them. I couldn't quite imagine what I would do with my own personal stylist, any more than I'd know what to do with my own personal butler; still, it was a nice little fantasy to indulge in for a bit.

Luke was such a gent, introducing me to everyone like he was at some cocktail party. They all seemed to know each other; maybe it's some sort of rock star club they all belong to. The organisers had agreed to our doing 'A Little Time', and had given us dancers and backing singers and the whole bit. It was a big production and I decided to treat it like an acting master class. Luke looked a bit embarrassed when I did more than just stand there and sing, but he could see the production people liked it and so he didn't complain. It worked OK with him singing it straight and me stamping back and forth around him, being really girly about the whole thing. It was cute. It felt good and the crowd whooped and yelled for more – but then they did that for all the numbers, being hyped up on a mixture of drink, drugs and encouragement from the management, who wanted the whole thing to look like a really happening event, not some dry industry thing.

After our set everyone backstage became even more friendly, like I had passed some sort of initiation test, become a member of their exclusive club. Luke was high on adrenalin, bouncing about like a kid in need of Ritalin. It was such a high. He had some coke, which we used when we got to a club afterwards, and then we danced through the night, the centre of attention, feeling like we owned the whole world.

Luke and his management were bubbling with plans. They wanted us to go on tour together, break America, become the next Carpenters. The music in the club was so loud I hadn't the energy to talk back or do anything except throw my arms round Luke's neck and cover him in kisses. I didn't want to be the one to break the mood with practicalities like my contract with *The Towers* and wanting to do the acting and all the exciting plans Dora had for me.

I even got to meet the famous Quentin James, although I can't say I warmed to the guy in his sharp blue suit, Hermès tie and shiny white shirt. To be honest, there seemed to be a whiff of sulphur in the air when he was around. Everyone else was treating me like I was one of them, but he seemed to be talking to me like some sarcastic old schoolmaster. I might have taken more offence if I hadn't noticed he did it to everyone.

'You need to cash in now,' he told me, leaning close in order to shout over the noise. 'I could make you a couple of million if you want to sell your story in the next few weeks.'

'Nah, I'm all right, thanks,' I shouted, wanting to be polite because he scared me a bit, but keen for him to piss off and leave me alone.

'Leave it too long and I can't promise I'll be able to get you anything. The public have short memories.'

'That's what I'm hoping,' I joked, but he didn't laugh, just looked irritated. He was so immaculate I just wanted to ruffle his hair, or make a smudge on one of his white cuffs. It looked to me like he was wearing some sort of foundation, which made him appear a bit orange, but maybe it was just a carefully applied tan. He had definitely had his teeth fixed – they looked like they would glow in the dark.

'It's up to you.' He shrugged, like he didn't have time for such foolishness. 'I can't make you do the right thing, I can only advise.'

'Thanks for the advice,' I said, snuggling up close to Luke, who seemed to be a bit in awe of the man but put his arm round me anyway as Quentin just walked off without so much as a goodbye.

'What a wanker,' I shouted into Luke's ear.

'A useful man to know when you need a few quid really quickly,' one of the other girls at the table said. 'Everyone ends up in his office eventually.' That was the second time someone had said that to me.

It was a great night and I wanted to indulge myself, and Luke, to the hilt. I was living the fantasy, riding the wave, dancing on top of the world till my thighs ached.

The next morning, when we woke up in a suite at the Covent Garden Hotel, I didn't feel half so good. In fact, I felt like complete crap. If I had stuck to the coke it wouldn't have been a problem, but in my euphoria, believing I could handle anything that life might throw at me, I'd also siphoned in an explosive mixture of free cocktails – pink ones, blue ones, crystal-clear ones – with no idea what was in any of them. It felt like someone had buried an axe between my eyes.

Luke must have been drinking water or something all night, because he was sitting on the other side of the room eating a cooked breakfast and reading the papers. If I felt bad when I woke up, I felt a fuck of a lot worse once he'd showed me the pictures of myself coming out of the club in the middle of the night. I had no memory of any of it, but it was definitely me, even though I looked more like Dad after one of his major benders, the ones that left him in the gutter outside the pub, waiting for Mum or one of us to scrape him up and stagger home with him.

Even though I was in too much pain to see the funny side of it myself at that moment, I did think Luke might at least crack a smile as he showed me, but he looked furious, like I'd let him down or something, shown myself up for the drunken slapper I really was. Worse still, he actually managed to make me feel guilty, made worse when I had to rush to the bathroom and get rid of the remains of the cocktails still swilling about in my stomach. Hauling myself up from where

I was, kneeling on the floor, I stared blearily into the mirror, shocked by the smeared make-up, crushed hair and deadly pallor that glowered back at me. I locked the door quickly and ran a shower, determined to improve things before I re-presented myself to the love of my life, who was looking so spruced up and clean living.

Eventually, having managed to at least get rid of the smell of sick, even though I hadn't managed to find any mascara to make my eyes look like they actually existed, I ventured back out, grabbing a pair of Ray-Bans he'd left on the side and ramming them over my eyes before sinking into the chair opposite him and accepting the cup of tepid black coffee he passed over. Finally he seemed unable to keep up the angry schoolmaster act any longer and cracked a grin.

'You look well and truly fucked,' he chuckled.

'Thanks.'

'I'll order some fresh coffee. You need your wits about you because we need to make plans.'

'Plans?'

'We need to think about the tour and everything else we talked about last night.'

Vaguely, through the haze of pain, I could recall snatches of the previous night.

'OK,' I said, a bit doubtfully. 'But we need to talk to Dora because she knows everything I'm going to be doing this year acting-wise.'

'Listen, babes,' he said, 'you are going to have to put the acting on hold for now. After last night we are really hot and you have to strike at moments like this. If we wait even six

135

months we will lose the momentum. Believe me, I know this business. It's all down to timing. You can go back to acting any time.'

I probably should have taken things a bit more slowly and tactfully at that stage, but my stomach was bubbling back up towards my throat again and I just didn't have the time for it.

'I've told you,' I said as I struggled back to my feet. 'Singing is just a hobby. The acting has to come first.'

'Don't let me down on this, Steff,' he said and I caught a glimpse of his face before I crashed back through the bathroom door. To look at him you'd have thought I'd just run him over with a truck.

Chapter Twelve

Since I hardly got to see Mum any more, at least not for long enough periods to really confide anything to her, Dora had become like my confessor. She seemed to be endlessly patient, just lighting one cigarette after another and pouring the coffee as I told her all about everything that had happened at the Brits and my worries about how it was getting out of control.

'Now Luke wants to go on tour and God knows what else,' I gabbled, a bit hysterical really. 'But I don't know.'

'The record company want you to do some songs on your own,' she said, as casually as if she'd just remembered a phone message she'd taken for me.

'You're kidding.' I felt a strange mixture of buzz and dread. 'He'd do his fucking nut if he knew that.'

'You're bigger than he is, Steff, and a better singer. Maybe he's going to have to face up to that. Where would Cher be if she'd stuck with Sonny?'

'Who?'

'Exactly.'

'How can I be bigger than Luke? What about the West End Boys and all those platinum records?'

'That was then. Just because the group was big doesn't mean he can be a star on his own. You're the one everyone's in love with now. And you've got a real talent. That's why he needs to be part of a double act with you. He had his chance on his own and it didn't work.'

'He's still famous,' I protested, a bit feebly.

'Only because of the band. Your generation of girls will always remember because you were fans, but younger kids won't have a clue who he is, any more than you could name the members of The Monkees or The Bay City Rollers.'

'Really? Jesus, if Luke ever thought that, it would destroy him. Singing is his whole life. I've already insulted him by suggesting acting is superior in some way.'

'He's a big boy now.' Dora shrugged. 'He knows how the business works. He's got to accept it.'

I couldn't get my head round that; I mean, he's Luke Lewis, for God's sake! To me he was always going to be a pop god. So I changed the subject. 'You ever heard of someone called Quentin James?'

'Of course, why?'

'He said I should sell my story. Said he could make me a couple of million.'

It was hard to believe I was even saying that. I mean, what sort of money is two million? It's like gigantic wealth, isn't it, and I was bandying the figures about like I was talking about a couple of hundred quid. Everything was going so weird.

'He probably could,' Dora said, in exactly the same matter-of-fact voice. 'He's very good at his job. All the editors take his

138

calls and he's set up most of the big deals in recent years. Everyone ends up in his office eventually.'

That bloody sentence again!

'Do you think I should do that?' I asked.

She paused for a moment to light a new cigarette and give herself time to think. She likes her dramatic pauses, does Dora. 'What you've got to ask yourself is: do the real stars sell their stories? I mean, the legends? Or is it just the little people? The big people may write their autobiographies, keeping control of every word that goes out, but do they actually go to the newspapers with their hands out for cash? Or do they retain their distance and their dignity? Apparently, the Royal Family have a saying: "Never apologise, never explain." You could do worse than take a leaf out of their book. Doing a deal with Quentin is like selling your soul to the devil. Once you've sold your story to one paper, all the others will see it as an invitation to discredit you in any way they can to try to get a slice of the cake. They'll make stuff up if necessary, just to get back at the paper you've done the deal with. At the moment you still have your integrity and dignity intact. Is it worth two million to lose that?'

I have to hand it to Dora, she has a way of putting things. Did I want to sell my soul for two million quid? Not such an easy question to answer, really.

I decided not to mention her comment about going solo to Luke. I had no intention of doing anything about it anyway and it would just have upset him, but that decision proved to be a mistake because three days later there was a story in one of the tabloids about men who were overshadowed by the

women in their lives – Prince Philip, Denis Thatcher, Guy
Ritchie and poor old Luke among them. The journalist
mentioned the rumour about me going solo as evidence that
I was 'eclipsing' Luke. I then made my second mistake when
I went round to his flat and he started raving about treachery
and whatever.

'I'm not going to go solo,' I assured him.

'So you knew about this?'

'Dora mentioned it.' I immediately knew I was in even
more trouble.

'And you didn't think you should tell me? Thanks a lot.'

'Oh fuck off, Luke. I didn't think anything of it, and I didn't
want to hurt your feelings. There was no need because I
wasn't going to do anything about it.'

The more I said the worse it got, the hole growing deeper
and deeper as I dug. I could see there was no easy way to get
myself out of it now, so I tried going quiet and just being
sweet, but he wasn't having any of it. His manhood had been
questioned, not to mention his talent, and it was more than he
could handle. Every petty resentment that he had been
building up inside against me – the record company, the
business in general, the other members of West End Boys,
their former management – all came pouring out. It was like
everyone in the world was conspiring against him, trying to
ruin his career. It was the sort of paranoid rant some junkie
might go into on a bad day. I kept quiet for a bit, but it was
like he was goading me, trying to force a reaction, make me
say something terrible and eventually I did.

I guess there must be a fair bit of Dad's temper lurking

inside me somewhere because I lost my patience and flared up, telling him not to be such a fucking wuss and to be happy that I loved him, that I didn't care whether he had number one records or not, that it was him I cared for not his fucking talent. Wrong thing to say again, apparently; I might as well have told him straight out he was a talentless nobody.

Realising my mistake I tried changing tack, telling him how talented he was, reminding him how much I'd loved his music when I was a kid. Well, that finally did it. Not only was I calling him talentless, I was telling him he was a has-been, over the hill, lucky to have someone as hot as me as a girlfriend. At that stage I lost all hope of being able to pull the whole thing back from the brink. In fact, I lost the will to even try.

I stormed out of his flat, bursting with anger, but by the time the taxi had delivered me back to my house the anger had been replaced by a terrible feeling of emptiness and desolation; an awareness that the best relationship of my life had just disintegrated in front of my eyes. Starting a relationship with Luke had been like another of my childhood dreams coming true, and now it had vanished as quickly as it had arrived. It felt horrible that I wasn't even going to be able to see his family to say goodbye properly. They had been a big part of the last few months of my life and with next to no contact from home they were pretty much all I had apart from Dora.

Maybe, I tried to tell myself, it was for the best. If my feelings for Luke had just been an extension of a childhood fantasy, perhaps it wasn't the most grown-up basis for a relationship. Was this the moment when I had to grow up and realise that dreams didn't always come true, even for someone enjoying a run of luck like mine?

All the way home the taxi driver insisted on chatting about *The Towers*, telling me everything about it that he hated. At the time, feeling trapped and unable to think straight, I just wanted to scream at him to shut up, but in fact he did me a favour by distracting me. At moments like that I hated the fact that people like him knew so much about my life and my work, or at least thought they did, while I knew nothing about them. I didn't know if he was the kind of guy who beat his wife and children, or anything about him. How come he was free to tell me about my life?

The moment I was inside the house I pulled all the curtains, not wanting anyone to be able to look in, and poured myself a vodka and Coke, adding an extra couple of slugs of vodka in the hope of speeding up a lift in my mood. I tried to fill the silence with the television, but the upbeat tones that seemed to come from every channel grated on my nerves and I had to turn the sound down low, just keeping the flickering picture for company. I tried ringing Mum but her phone was switched off, so I left a message. I tried my sisters and got through but they were in a hurry to go because they were getting ready to go out. There was nothing I could have said to them anyway – they didn't know anything about my relationship with Luke. How could I complain to them about anything in my life when they believed I'd had all the lucky breaks that they would have wanted? I poured myself another drink, my mood still not lifting, but the pain beginning to numb a little.

When my phone went off, I just picked it up and answered

without checking who it was. I don't know why I did that. I never usually did. I suppose I just assumed it would be Luke or Mum.

'Hi, Steffi, Quentin James here.'

'How did you get this number?' That came out too sharply, but I was past caring about politeness. Had he heard about the split with Luke already? Was there nothing this bloody man didn't know about?

'No one can escape me,' he chuckled, in a voice that I guess was supposed to sound jokey but actually came across as spooky. 'I think we need to meet.'

'No, really,' I said, the vodka making me bold, 'I truly don't want to sell my story to the papers.'

I was even more certain of that having seen the damage my career choices so far had done to my private life. My father was refusing to speak to me ever again and now the love of my life had dumped me. The last thing I needed was to raise my profile any further.

'Well, as you know, I think you're wrong on that. But this is about something different. Someone else has come forward with a story that affects you and I thought I ought to give you a chance to hear it first.'

'I'm really not interested.' This was more than I could cope with. 'If it's another old school friend dishing the dirt then do your worst.'

A sudden, horrible thought struck me. 'Is it Luke?'

'No.' He paused and I realised I had accidentally given him a glimpse into my head. 'Why would it be Luke? Have you two fallen out?'

'No,' I said, too fast to be convincing. 'I don't want to be rude but I'm going to hang up because I really don't want to talk now.'

I hung up before he could protest, feeling rude but terrified I would give something else away if I kept talking. He tried to ring back but I ignored it, draining my drink then pouring myself another vodka, leaving out the Coke.

I didn't answer any more calls from unknown numbers, and there seemed to be an awful lot of them, although I was getting a bit confused and dropped the phone quite a few times as I squinted at it, trying to work out who kept ringing and ringing. Eventually I realised it was the doorbell not the phone and I staggered out to answer it. I hoped it would be Mum, responding to my message from earlier, or Luke, realising he'd made a mistake and wanting to make up. I don't know why I thought it was a good idea to open my door without checking at the peephole first, when I'd been going to so much trouble not to answer my phone, but there wasn't anything very logical going on in my brain by then. Maybe I just craved a bit of company, somebody to help me empty out the rest of the vodka. Maybe I tried to look but hadn't been able to focus my eyes properly by that stage.

Two complete strangers stood on the doorstep, a man and a woman. I could see they were startled by the state I was in. They announced they were from the *News of the World*. I was getting sick of hearing that name, and told them so. They didn't really seem to hear, but it's possible my words were a bit slurred by then and hard to make out. They said they'd been trying to get me by phone because they were following up a story. I tried really hard to understand what they were telling me. It sounded like they were saying a woman had come forward claiming she was my mother. Why would that be interesting to them? Mum wasn't exactly a state secret. Maybe it was to do with Dad smacking her about. I was about to ask them if that was the best they could do for a story this week, then thought better of it. The man on the doorstep was holding up a picture of a woman who looked like an actress, although I didn't recognise her. He was asking if I knew her.

I leaned forward and squinted really hard, but the effort made me lose my balance and I toppled into his arms, which really wasn't what I intended. My legs didn't seem to be responding very well and so they helped me back into the sitting room and laid me out on the sofa. That was a mistake, because I promptly threw up over the man's shoes – which should have been embarrassing, but for some reason I didn't seem to care about anything any more. I did, however, feel a bit better and had another go at trying to understand what they were going on about. They seemed to think that this woman in the photograph was my mother. I explained that she was the wrong colour for one thing – which made me laugh a lot, but not them – and that I had never seen her before in my life. After a while they seemed to accept that they were wasting their time. The female reporter left the woman's photograph on the table, and a card with her mobile number on, and said I could call her if I wanted to give an interview and that's the last thing I remember. I guess I must have passed out and they must have let themselves out of the house because by the time I woke up, probably around 14 hours later, there was no one else there.

The room was a pretty good mess and it looked like I had been sick a bit more in my sleep – most of the vomit had matted into my hair and dried to a crust on the sofa cushions. It took me a few moments to delve far enough back through the nauseous feelings before I remembered why I was so drunk and a dull emotional pain mixed in with all the others.

Little snatches of what had happened the previous night were beginning to come back to me. Seeing the picture of the woman on the table brought a vague memory back, but it wasn't clear. There was something familiar about her, but I couldn't work out what it was. I drank a glass of water, made myself some coffee and toast and sat down to stare at it.

After a while my curiosity got the better of me and I staggered out to the corner shop, collar turned up, Beanie hat pulled way down and Ray-Bans over the eyes, bought a paper, and hurried back home as quickly as possible in case any opportunist decided to take a picture. I guessed it was inevitable after my performance for the reporters that they would soon all be following up my 'problems with drink' story.

It had taken me a while to get to the stage of disguising myself when I went out. I didn't like doing it to start with because I thought it made it seem like I thought I was something important; who does she think she is, then, that she has to go around in disguise? I also quite liked being recognised, especially as everyone was always so friendly, and anyway it was Nikki they were talking to really, not me. But that had very quickly become the problem, because people talked dirty to Nikki, due to the fact that she was a bit of an unashamed slapper. I can talk as dirty as the next person, so it wasn't that I was shocked or anything, but it does get kind of boring when every bloody man you pass in the street shouts out one of a limited selection of jokes: 'Fancy a shag?', 'Any chance of a blow-job?', 'What can I get for a fiver?' – that sort of thing – obviously believing that he's the first person in the world to think of such a witty comment.

It became a bit less comfortable still when people started to get the hang of who Steffi was, and started talking to me rather than to Nikki. I know that sounds a bit daft, but it was the way I felt. I didn't mind answering back to questions like, 'How much for a blow-job?' or 'Fancy a quickie?' when I could kid myself I was just pretending to be Nikki, but it seemed a bit more personal when it was me; a bit threatening, if I'm honest. Some blokes have a way of letting you know that they really mean it too, that it isn't just a bit of blokish fun; they're the sort of guys you wouldn't ever want to be trapped with alone in a lift, if you know what I mean. There'd been a few of them around the estate when I was a kid, but there I could always avoid them. Now it felt like it was becoming harder to become invisible.

Once the revelations about the squat were published everything went up a notch. Anyone who had coughed up a few pence for a newspaper felt they had the right to talk to me about what they read in it. I guess there is some poetic justice in that, but it doesn't half get on your nerves after about the tenth time in a half-hour trip to the shops.

But it's not too hard to make yourself invisible if you don't mind looking a bit of a mess. In fact, it could be quite liberating to go out looking a bit dowdy and not getting any looks or catcalls. It makes me think I could get the hang of wearing those Muslim outfits where only the eyes are visible. Put one of those on and you can watch the world in private, invisible to them all, like looking out through the darkened glass of a limousine. I can see how that might become a bit comfortable, but maybe not if you have to do it all the time.

Anyway, I managed to get back to the house with the newspapers without a single person giving me a second look, and without throwing up my toast and coffee.

It was still quite tricky to concentrate on the print without the room starting to spin around again and the nausea rising back up, but it wasn't hard to spot the offending article. There was a headline right across the front page, advertising the story inside: 'Steffi's real mum steps out of the past'.

'Oh my God,' I thought, 'what kind of fuckery is this?' (Thank you, Amy Winehouse, for the invention of the perfect phrase to fit so many situations.)

I found the page they were talking about, with the same woman's face staring out of it. The headlines were big enough for me to be able to digest them without too much effort, but beyond that it was just a mass of dirty grey print.

There were four whole pages of it, with big pictures of this silly old tart posing for the cameras like she was still a teenager, pouting and fluttering her eyelashes. There were old pictures too, from when she actually was young and pretty, which looked like they were from the 1970s, all platform shoes and weird hair. Who the fuck was she?

The pictures made it look like she thought she was some sort of celebrity but I'd never heard of her. I tried to read the text, but the words didn't seem to make sense to me. My eyes were bleary with tears and I was having trouble getting enough air, which was making me feel faint and sick at the same time. I stopped for a moment, took some deep breaths and stared out the window, but when I looked back down my eyes had gone even more out of focus. It was like this woman and the reporter she was talking to had managed to climb into the very deepest, darkest, most private part of me. They were attacking Mum and Dad and the very core of who I was. There was even a fuzzy old picture of Dad, looking a lot younger than I ever remembered, and a new picture of him peering out through the net curtains at home like some trapped animal or a seedy old criminal in hiding. The press must have had the flat under siege in order to get that shot and I knew how horrible that felt.

I remembered the reporters coming to see me; the woman's card was still lying on the table. I thought about ringing her and asking her what the fuck she thought she was doing making up such a bloody stupid load of crap, but I stopped myself. The tiny bit of common sense that was still able to function among the flood of adrenalin told me that I needed to have at least read the whole story before I started sounding off. I also knew that if I rang then I would lose my temper and end up in floods of tears, which would not be helpful.

Although I couldn't concentrate enough to read the main part of the text, I could make out some of the bits they had

149

extracted and put into bigger print, and I could read the captions under the pictures. She seemed to be saying that she'd had an affair with Dad, got pregnant and that Mum had agreed to bring me up as her own. She also seemed to be claiming that giving me away had broken her heart, which was why she had never been able to make contact with me again.

Part of me wanted to laugh at the ridiculousness of it, but another part immediately thought how hurt and upset Mum would be by such a horrible story. I reached for the phone and dialled her number, but it was switched off. Things were beginning to feel bad. I really needed to speak to her, to explain that this was nothing to do with me, to apologise for bringing all this to their door, to tell her how much I loved her. I plucked up my courage and dialled the home number. Dad answered, the first time I'd heard his voice since he'd phoned to say I was no daughter of his and never would be again.

'Can I speak to Mum, please?' I asked, fighting to keep my voice steady.

He hung up. I rang back, angry now, but the phone just kept ringing. I could imagine him shouting at everyone not to answer it, that it was just that bitch of a non-daughter who had brought disgrace on the whole family. I had never felt so alone in my life. Part of me wanted to ring Luke, but a small stubborn streak – inherited from Dad, I guess – wouldn't let me be the first one to make contact there. Dora's phone was switched off and I couldn't think of anyone else. Then I saw Gerry's name and dialled without thinking, knowing he would be pleased to hear from me, feeling safe, feeling guilty that I was turning to him like this in my hour of need.

'Hi, Gerry, it's me.'

'Are you OK?' he asked. I wondered if he'd seen the paper or if he could just tell from my voice.

'No. Can you come over?'

'Of course. I'll be there in ten minutes.'

Gerry had been on my conscience a bit. He was always so nice to me around the studio, never putting me under any pressure, even though it was obvious how he felt about me, but always happy to chat in the canteen or during the quiet bits of the day when we were all waiting for something to happen. I'd taken to reading books a lot during the quiet periods and he always seemed to have read them all and remembered all the plots and characters.

'I had to travel a lot before I got this gig,' he'd reminded me, 'doing documentaries up mountains and in jungles and the rest. You get a lot of time to read when you're on planes or lying awake in tents listening to insects.'

I was really getting into all the telly 'classics', things like *Jane Eyre* and *Pride and Prejudice*. I fancied doing some of those, sitting around in posh houses in pretty costumes twittering about husbands and the rest. I wanted something that would show I could do the posh accent, that I wasn't just doing Nikki well because she sounded like me.

Some of the other actors read a lot too, but others would tease me for being a boffin, a bit like my family might have done or my friends at school, but more good natured. That was pretty much the extent of my relationship with Gerry since I'd moved out of his house and I was worried that I might be using him by only calling on him now I was completely alone and confused. I needn't have worried – the moment he arrived it was obvious he was happy to be asked and was only concerned by how upset he could see I was. The ease with which he wore his friendship for me made me want to cry all over again.

I made us both a cup of tea while he read the article in silence. By the time I plonked the mug down beside him he'd read as much as he needed to.

'And this is truly the first you've heard of any of this?' he asked.

'Absolutely. Quentin James, you know, the publicity guy, he warned me there was going to be a story coming out, but I just ignored him. I mean, there are stories coming out all the time; I didn't think one more would make much difference. Then these reporters came round to get my reaction but I was too wasted to be able to understand what they were saying.'

It felt like I'd gone into shock, numbed by the enormity of this woman's claim. Was she a lunatic? If so, how had she managed to convince the newspaper of such an unlikely story? Or was it that they didn't even care if it was likely or not, as long as it sold newspapers? So many questions and absolutely no answers in sight.

My phone was ringing constantly and I checked to see who each of the callers was in case it was Mum or Luke, but neither came up on the screen. There were a lot of numbers I didn't recognise but guessed must be the press, and then Quentin James's name came on. I didn't even know his number was in my phone, which was a bit spooky, like he was stalking me. He must have put it in there himself at some stage when I wasn't looking, maybe in some club somewhere when I was too drunk to take in what was going on. I hesitated for a second and then picked up.

'Hi,' he said, without even bothering to confirm it was him speaking, which seemed a bit of a presumption – one more presumption in a long fucking line. 'Seen the paper?'

'Yes,' I said, having abandoned the idea of trying to act cool and pretend I hadn't. 'It's complete bullshit. She must be some sort of con artist. Or did you put her up to it? Is she one of your sad fucking clients, hoping to get a bit of cheap publicity?'

'She's one of my clients, and I've checked her out like I check out everyone who comes to me. The story stands up. She is your real mum.'

'That is such crap!' The tears rose up and threatened to block my throat. I felt Gerry squeezing my hand.

'Why don't you come and meet her at my office tomorrow?' Quentin suggested, all reasonable and fatherly.

'I'm working tomorrow,' I snapped.

'Come after work. You tell me the time and I'll get her here.'

My first instinct was to tell him to fuck off, but I was actually kind of intrigued to meet a woman who would make up a story like this. If I met her, I reasoned, maybe she wouldn't seem so threatening; maybe she would just turn out to be a bit of a hopeless loon and I would be able to force Quentin to sort the whole mess out, issue an apology, whatever it was that they did in these cases.

I agreed to do it and he promised to text me the address. I felt bad to be even talking to such a slimeball, but it seemed that there was no way round it just at the moment. Gerry promised to go with me. I wasn't sure that I would have been able to handle such a stroll into the lion's den without him there.

Several hours later, I got a call from Mum. I guess she'd had to wait until Dad was out of the house, down the pub. I could tell she'd been crying.

'I'm so sorry, baby,' she said, her voice choking up.

'There's nothing for you to be sorry about,' I said. 'I'm sorry I've brought all these fucking lunatics out of the woodwork.'

'I'm sorry that you had to find out like this.'

That stopped me in my tracks as effectively as a punch in the face.

Chapter Thirteen

Gerry could see I was in shock and put his arm around me. I didn't seem to be able to stop myself from shaking, like I was coming down from a bad trip, or staggering out of a car crash. I just couldn't get things straight in my head.

'She says it's true,' I managed to say eventually.

'Shit.' He hung on to me for a minute, then said, 'We need to get you out of here before the rest of the press arrive.'

'Where can I go? I could go to a hotel, I suppose.'

'No.' He sounded firm, calm, in control. 'We'll go to Mum and Dad's. No one will think of looking for you there.'

'What about your neighbours?' I asked, remembering the video camera at the bedroom window outside my house the night Pete came round.

'I don't even know who the neighbours are,' he admitted. 'Mum and Dad have always pretty much kept themselves to themselves. As long as you aren't seen going in, we'll be fine. No one would think of connecting you to us.'

The idea of being anonymous again, like Gerry and his family, seemed incredibly attractive. I had always thought that being famous was the passport to everything good in life, not realising it would mean never being able to escape from anyone who might be looking for me.

From a quick glimpse at my reflection in the mirror I could see it was unlikely anyone was going to recognise me from a casual glance just at the moment. To be honest I looked like a complete minger, and if anyone did manage to get a picture it would make the front pages just because it showed what a state I'd got myself into. The press were still trying to get through on the phone, but when Gerry peered out there was no sign of any activity yet in the street. I shoved a few essentials into a bag, drew the rest of the curtains so they wouldn't know whether I was there or not, and we scurried down the road to Gerry's battered old Saab. I glanced up at the bedroom opposite but there was no one there. He'd be kicking himself if he knew what he was missing, the nosey bastard.

When we got there it felt a bit like coming home. Gerry's mum and dad were so sweet, just acting like it was a normal Sunday and I was just a normal girlfriend that their son was bringing home for a visit. They were *Sunday Express* readers, not *News of the World*, so they hadn't heard anything about this latest twist in my parallel tabloid life. Going there was exactly the right thing to do, just to be having a normal Sunday at home with a normal family. Gerry was so kind to me, not trying to force me to talk if I didn't want to, just making sure I had food and warmth and an endless river of hot tea.

As the shock of the revelations began to wear off and the shaking died down, I found I could actually read the story and take it in. The woman's name was Maggie, although she might have been making that up because her whole life seemed to be a bit of a sham. The story was that she had been a bit of a 'vice girl' herself in the 1970s and 1980s (their words, not mine, and probably not hers either, I guess, knowing how reporters work). She claimed she'd had a one-night stand with Dad when they met in a strip club in Soho when Dad was on a stag night with some mates.

That was a pretty revolting picture to get my head round, but I managed to do it without losing the little bit of lunch that I'd managed to choke down. She then went into a whole load of crap about how she had to give me up because of the stigma of being an unmarried mother in 'those days' and the pressures of society – I mean, we're hardly talking about Victorian times here, are we? It was the late bloody 1980s, for fuck's sake! Seemed more likely it was the pressures of being a career 'vice girl' that helped her towards her decision, but I kept telling myself I shouldn't judge the woman on things I read in the press because it was impossible to know which were her own words and which ones had been put into her mouth by reporters. She did say that giving me up to Mum had been 'the most painful day of her life'. Well, good!

Mum came across as pretty much a saint in the whole thing – if perhaps a bit of a doormat to Dad – and the paper didn't hesitate to remind its readers of how I had told my acting class about Dad beating her up. I felt really sorry for her, but I was also beginning to feel a bit pissed off with her as well. If even part of this woman's story was true, how come Mum had never told me? How had she let me go on believing she was my mum for so long? Why wasn't she ringing me and coming round and helping me to come to terms with things, explaining the story from her side? Unless, of course, Dad wasn't letting her. That was likely, but why was she letting him do that to both of us? Why didn't she stand up to him for once? I loved her like mad, but I had to admit she was coming out of this looking like a bit of a serial victim.

It also pissed me off to think that Dad had been lecturing me about the family's 'reputation', when he had pulled a stunt like this. How dare he refuse to talk to me when he'd been lying to me all these years? If I was endangering the family's good name by being an actress, what was he doing that night in Soho?

The more I thought about the whole situation the more my head was spinning. Most of all I felt like I'd been isolated even further from the family. If the story was true, my brothers and sisters didn't even share the same mother as me. I truly was an outsider.

Gerry came to bed with me that night, but he didn't even attempt sex, just cuddled me until my whirling thoughts finally allowed me to go to sleep. I was grateful for that. My head was still full of Luke and it wouldn't have felt right to be doing it with someone else – not yet. Not even Gerry.

The next morning we set off for the studios together like an old married couple, falling back into our old routine. There were a few press lurking around outside the studio doors, but they didn't even give a second glance to the scruffy young couple in the battered old car. As the day progressed they started to find ways of getting through to me inside the studio, despite security. One got into the canteen at lunchtime, posing as an actor on some other programme; another managed to get me paged on the studio landline by pretending to be calling about my grandmother dying. A third got through to my mobile when someone else answered it for me while I was filming. They were all making the same offers of protection if I sold them my side of the story. I said nothing to any of them, just pretended I couldn't hear them, as if they didn't exist. I can understand now how film stars or other people in the media get that glazed look in their eyes when they're walking through crowds. They have to make the outside world invisible otherwise it would overwhelm them with its attentions. I don't know why I'm talking about them like they're another species; I had become one of them and it was a very scary feeling. At least film stars have their millions to protect them, and their studio minders, and the big politicians have policemen at their doors. All I had between me and the pack was Gerry and his mum and dad.

The whole day I had a lot of trouble concentrating on work, which worried me. I had a big scene to do with one other character, just the two of us, spitting and fighting over the same man – Nikki had been up to her tricks with someone else's husband and the shit was just hitting the fan. We did take after take and in the end I just had to summon every ounce of energy and block everything else out of my mind. I really let rip, which had the desired effect, taking my fellow actress by surprise, which worked for the scene. The crew gave me a round of applause at the end, which made me feel good for about ten seconds before I remembered what I was going to be doing that evening after work.

I was still very unclear what I was in for once I got to Quentin James's office. Mum had been too choked up to really explain anything over the phone, and then Dad must have come back into the room she was calling from because she suddenly pretended to be talking to someone else and hung up, all breezy and cheerful; I was coming to the conclusion she was a better actress than I had previously given her credit for. A few days earlier I would have assumed that was where I'd inherited my talent from, but now I didn't know anything any more. That was what was really freaking me out. Who the fuck was I? Was Dad really my dad? Was I adopted? I hadn't been able to get any questions out during the call and when I tried to ring back again later her phone had been turned off. Chances were he'd guessed who she was talking to and had smashed it to pieces. If he was cross with me before, he must have been a thousand times angrier by then and just thinking about it made me want to cry again.

Gerry was really sweet with me all day, just being there, not asking any questions, just waiting for me to talk to him. At the end of filming he walked out of the studio with me without saying a word. I slid my hand into his and squeezed tightly.

Quentin's offices in Soho were full of posh girls on phones, but weren't half as flash as I would have expected. It looked like a place where work actually got done and posing was kept to an absolute minimum. Not that Quentin wasn't a hell of a poser himself, and I had to allow him a bit of a gloat since he had warned me that there was a big story coming and had offered to help me out (with a good dollop of self-interest there as well). Quentin's own office was a complete tip, filled with piles of magazines and newspapers and a giant television screen; the mess made me feel slightly more kindly disposed towards him. As we walked past what looked like a conference room I noticed there was a film camera crew working in there. A year before I would have paid a bit more attention, but I no longer found the presence of cameras remarkable; in fact, it sometimes felt quite strange when there weren't any around.

'Welcome to the lion's den,' Quentin joked, shaking my hand and entirely ignoring Gerry, which seemed a bit bloody rude but not worth making a point about just yet. I really wanted to find out as much as possible about this woman who claimed to be my mother, and if that meant I had to be polite to Quentin for a bit I was willing to swallow that. Gerry was just going to have to put up with it. He didn't seem remotely bothered, but then he never seemed remotely bothered about anything really.

'I'm so glad you've come,' Quentin purred. 'I think we can help you a lot.'

'I don't really understand what's going on,' I admitted.

'Well, luckily for you, I do,' he beamed smugly, 'because this is my business. You, my dear, have become part of the great national pantomime; one of the characters that the public want to see up on the media stage every day and, in order to satisfy that need, the media will be looking for any stories they can find about you, and when they can't find any they will make them up.'

'I already know that.'

'I'm sure you do, but this is probably just the beginning. With our help you can take control of which stories get out there, and we can limit the damage of the unauthorised ones that manage to slip through the net. As much of my time is spent keeping stories about my clients out of the papers as getting the stories they want in.'

He appeared to be taking it for granted that I was there to take him on as my own personal publicist, which seemed about as wise a course of action as recruiting a pimp to set me up on a blind date. I decided not to disillusion him until I had got as much information out of him as possible.

'They've decided that you are a "tart with a heart" – a cliché, I know, but the whole pantomime is cast on the basis of cliché: cliché villains; cliché heroes; cliché fallen women; cliché love rats. Once you've been allotted your role it's hard to change it, unless they decide to recast you. That's when you hear people moaning on about: "The media built me up, then they decided to destroy me." The general public likes a Greek tragedy. We like our gods to be shown to have feet of clay. But that doesn't mean they don't still love you.'

He was getting bloody comfortable on his hobby horse and I tuned out, taking a bit more of an interest in what was going on in the conference room, which I could sort of make out through the series of glass partitions that divided the floor up. There was a woman sitting at the conference table, talking to camera, wreathed in cigarette smoke. After a moment or two she stubbed her fag out and the fog cleared slightly.

'Is that her?' I asked, my voice croaking like an old frog.

'Yes,' Quentin said and for a second he seemed to be lost for words, like he might actually have been caught out on something.

'I thought smoking in offices was illegal.'

'Special dispensation on emotional grounds,' he grinned, as if the two of us were sharing an in-joke. 'She would really like to meet you, you know.'

'Who are the camera crew?' Gerry asked.

Quentin ignored him, as if he hadn't spoken.

'Who are the camera crew?' I repeated.

'They're making a documentary about her, a reality make-over thing. It would be great to film you meeting her for the first time. It would be very compelling.'

'You're fucking joking, aren't you?' I couldn't believe his nerve.

'You feel like that now,' he went on, smooth as silk, 'but once the fuss has died down it will be nice to have something to look back on.'

'This isn't a family holiday. I'm not shifting from this office till you get that camera crew out.'

Quentin sat still for a moment, like an old lizard trying to out-stare me. I didn't flicker and he cracked first. 'OK, give me a minute.'

He went through to the boardroom and we could see him talking to the cameraman. Maggie glanced across at me and I didn't avert my eyes. She looked away nervously and fumbled around to find a fresh cigarette. She'd obviously done herself up for the cameras and looked quite striking, a bit like an old film star, but when I stared I could see things weren't quite as glamorous as the first impression.

The camera crew all left with their equipment and Quentin came back to get me. I took a grip of Gerry's hand, to make sure he knew I wanted him there for moral support, and walked through with my head held high. It looked for a second as if she was going to get up as we came in, but then she seemed to think better of it and stayed put – making herself look a bit arrogant, to be honest. She didn't put her hand out or anything, maybe afraid I would reject it, and just sat puffing on the fag, which made her look pretty in-your-face and not exactly maternal.

Close up she was a lot rougher than she had seemed from the other end of the office. She could have done with a bit more weight, her neck was scraggy and there was a line of make-up along her chin, like she was wearing a kabuki mask. Her skin had been smoked as dry as an old kipper, mapped with tiny lines she'd tried to cover with pancake, particularly around the mouth.

Her eyelids were drooping, which meant that the blue eye shadow she'd caked on them looked a bit grotesque in close-up. She looked like one of those women you see selling cosmetics in the department stores – not quite a real person any more. The photographer for the paper must have done a fair bit of touching up to make the pictures look even remotely attractive. She was wearing a lot of perfume too, but it didn't hide the stink of cigarettes, which clung to her like it clung to Dora.

'Steffi,' Quentin said, 'this is Maggie.'

'Hi,' Maggie said.

'Hi.'

I mean, what else was there to say? I stared hard at her. She did look very familiar. I wondered if she had been watching

164

me over the years, without me knowing, and I had seen her in the distance. Then I realised what it was: she looked like me. Oh my God! Beneath the wrinkles and sagging and brittle-looking hair was the face that stared at me from the mirror every day. It was hard to tell if the hair had always been dyed, but I was willing to bet that she had once been the same white blonde that I was.

'Would you guys like us to leave you alone?' Quentin asked.

'Yes,' she said.

'No!' I said, much more vehemently. I was nowhere close to being ready to spend one-on-one time with this old harridan. They all froze and the atmosphere became even edgier. I remained standing, looking down at her.

'What made you decide to speak out now?' I asked eventually.

'Quentin thought it would be a good idea,' she smirked, as if she and Quentin were the grown-ups in this situation, the insiders.

'What made you decide to come and see him, then?' I persevered, resisting the temptation to punch her.

'I needed advice on the best way to handle the situation. I wanted to make contact with you.'

I turned on Quentin. 'That was your advice? A woman comes to you saying she would like to make contact with the baby she gave away at birth and you suggest she does it through the *News of the World*?'

'Maggie is my client, I had to advise her what would be in her best interests. The story was worth more if there was a surprise factor. I did contact you, if you remember, but you didn't want to listen.'

'You really are gutter slime, aren't you?'

Now he was smirking too and I realised that he was impossible to insult. The man was so completely certain of his own rightness that nothing I could ever say to him would change his opinion of what he had done. In a way he was right, of course: he was just doing the job for his client.

'Money's a bit of a problem,' Maggie said. 'I'm getting to an age where I have to think about how I'm going to survive. Show business doesn't always provide a pension. You'll need to bear that in mind if you're going to stay in the business. You can be all high and mighty about it now, but you'll need the help of experts like Quentin if you don't want to end up in some home for retired beach donkeys one day.'

For a second I almost laughed at the image, then caught myself. Did this sad old slapper really think she was part of show business? Worse still, did she really think I was part of the same business as her? What about all that Shakespeare with Dave, and improvisation with Dora? What about all the scripts I'd read and the books and the plays I'd sneaked into when I could afford them? Had she done all that? Maybe she had, maybe this really was the way I was going to end up, and that was why Dad was so set against me going into the business. He knew exactly where I was heading because he'd seen it at first hand.

'I still don't get it,' I said.

She shrugged and picked an imaginary fleck of tobacco off her tongue. (I'm guessing it was imaginary because the cigarette was filtered.) 'I'm really proud of you,' she said, avoiding my eyes. 'I wanted you to know that.'

'Thanks,' I said and an awkward silence fell. 'I've got to go, I've got a meeting.'

It was obviously a lie, but none of them called me on it. We were all equally keen to escape from the room and breathe some clean air. As we came out, the television crew appeared in reception again. The cameraman had switched on and was pointing his lens at me without saying a word.

'Turn that fucking camera off or I'll kick your bollocks up between your ears!' I snarled as I walked past. Things, it seemed, were really starting to get to me.

Chapter Fourteen

Dora had arranged a meeting for me at the record company on my one day off from *The Towers* that week. I felt a bit of a fraud saying I had a record company – I mean, most musicians work for years to get anyone to even look at them while I'd swanned in on the back of one crappy television talent show that had given me a number-one novelty track. But it was still nice to have something to take my mind off all the other stuff and it was comforting to be with Dora and to just relax for an hour or two, being treated like I was a star, even if it was based on one freak Christmas hit.

'We've been doing a lot of brainstorming on where to place you in the market,' one of the suits told me once we were all comfortably sitting around in their flashy meeting room.

'The demographics are difficult to read,' another chimed in.

'Demographics?' Not a word I was completely sure about.

'Which sector of the market you are likely to appeal to,' Dora explained. '"Summer Wine" was bought by everyone from grannies to kids; it would be hard to repeat that sort of success next time. They want to work out who your core market of fans are likely to be and then target them.'

'Sounds a bit like a war plan,' I joked. 'Can't I just record a few good songs and see what happens?'

They all humoured me for a few minutes, but they obviously thought that was about the worst idea they'd ever heard. They kept telling me how wonderful the Brits performance was and how highly I had rated when they market-researched me with the public. They were talking about 'touring' and 'breaking America' and God knows what else and I began to feel a bit sick because I knew I didn't want to do any of it. I wished Luke was there because it had all seemed more fun when it was just him and me and a stupid television talent show. This all seemed a bit serious and was likely to cost everyone a ton of money. He would have known what to say to them, but at the same time I knew he would have been agreeing to everything they suggested, so maybe it was better he wasn't there. Touring America with the West End Boys had been one of the highlights of his life and I knew that was one of the reasons he was pissed off with me. He had been hoping to relive his glory days again with me. I felt so bad about letting him down, but it just wasn't something I felt comfortable with. I still missed him all the time, still hoped that every call would turn out to be him. And I still wasn't going to be the first one to crack and make the call.

One of the executives wanted me to write my own material, like I needed another hobby just at the moment, while another executive suggested I record some classic cover versions.

'Connie Francis!' someone else yelped, like they'd just discovered gravity. 'Well overdue for a remix. Fantastic, moving stuff!'

And so it went on, round and round and round, part fantasy, part hard-nosed businessmen desperately trying to find a concept they could get hold of and market to death. When it was all over, they offered to take us to dinner, but I'd had enough by then and said I had somewhere else to go.

'That was a lie,' I admitted to Dora once we were safely back out in the real world. 'Can you and I go somewhere? I'm starving. I'll pay.'

It felt nice to be able to say that. The money had finally started to filter through and I was able to make gestures like that without even thinking about it. I'd been sending money home to Mum as well, which felt even better.

'Sure, where would you like to go?'

'I don't care. Nothing flashy. Chinese, maybe.'

We headed for Chinatown and chose one that was shielded from the street and had booths so I could disappear. None of the staff gave any sign of recognising me, even though *The Towers* was playing on a television in the corner of the room and Nikki was in full flow, screaming abuse at one of her punters. Maybe we all look the same to them. (Only joking, honest.)

'So, how are you really?' Dora asked once we'd ordered and had a bottle of wine on the table.

'A bit stressed to be honest.'

'This Maggie woman, is she really your birth mother?'

'I think she must be. No one is exactly denying it, and when I met her I thought I could see a family resemblance, although she's let herself go a bit.'

'How did she fall into Quentin James's clutches?' Dora gave a little shiver as she mentioned his name. He seemed to have that effect on a lot of people: part admiration and part revulsion.

'She's hard up, I think, and wants one last stab at making it.'

'Funny idea of "making it". What does your mum say about it all?'

'I haven't been able to get hold of her. I think Dad must have taken her phone or something.'

'It would be good to talk it over with her, wouldn't it?'

'I'm a bit pissed off with her, to be honest. I mean, why didn't she ever say anything?'

'Maybe she hoped you would never need to know. If it's all true, she acted pretty nobly. I mean, you never got any idea from her that you weren't just like all her other children, did you?'

'No. Actually I sometimes thought I was her favourite. But she was good at making us all feel like that, I think.'

'So maybe you are going to have to think about forgiving her.'

I didn't reply. Too much was going on in my head.

'And what about Luke?' she pressed on. 'Is that really all over?'

I felt a nasty stab of pain in my chest at her words. 'It seems like it. He was starting to be really funny about it all.'

She nodded, as if she'd seen such things a million times before. 'And Gerry?'

'He's so sweet, and such a good friend, and Mum thinks he's absolutely lovely, but ...'

'But he's not Luke.'

I nodded, sitting back to let the waitress lay out the hotplates in readiness for the food.

'So, what did you think about the things they were all saying at the meeting?' she asked.

'I don't know,' I sighed. 'I mean it all sounds fun, but I don't want to be a pop singer if it means I have to give up the acting, and I doubt if it's possible to do both justice.'

'Billie Piper made the transition well. Cher got a best actress Oscar and she started out as a singer. Diana Ross, Whitney, J-Lo, Beyoncé ...'

'Yeah, yeah, I get the message, but being a pop princess almost killed Billie Piper and you know what everyone says about Whitney ... I just don't want to push my luck; getting *The Towers* was a good break. Nikki's made me a household name. If I went out on the road flogging records I would be just like all the rest of them.'

'Nice to be in a position to have such a dilemma.'

'I know, I know. I'm sorry. Am I behaving like a spoiled brat?'

'Not at all. It's very refreshing, and you're right. Lots of girls can sing nicely but not many can act like you.'

'Oh, I don't know,' I tried to change the subject. 'I've just had some lucky breaks, like coming to your classes.'

'Lots of people have found my classes in the past, but none had the potential you have. Only a few people as talented as you come along in each generation. We should probably be thinking about getting you *Hedda Gabler* at the National rather than *Sweet Charity*.'

'Can't I do both?'

'Probably,' she laughed, 'if you play it right.'

'Play it?'

'The fame game. Schmoozing with the right people, not losing your credibility, all that.'

'Sounds like a day out on a tightrope.'

'It will be. You've seen that already.'

The rest of the evening passed in a bit of a haze as I demolished most of the bottle of wine. I wasn't due at the studio until the afternoon the next day because we had a night shoot to do on location, so I was still sleeping it off when the house phone started to ring the next morning. Hardly anyone used the landline, so I dragged myself up from my dreams and picked it up.

'Sorry,' Dora's voice drawled into my ear, 'did I wake you?'

'Don't worry. What time is it?'

'About nine. I just rang so I could say, "I told you so."'

'Ah.' I struggled to work out what she was on about. 'OK.'

'Ask me what I was right about this time.'

'OK, what were you right about this time?'

'Your acting ability. I've just had a call from Bafta. You're up for an award.'

'I am?'

'Best actress.'

'Fucking hell.'

'Look out, Oscar, here comes Steffi.'

Good old Dora, always there to dangle the dream a little bit further out of my reach.

The full impact of her words didn't hit me until after I'd hung up the phone. Best actress? That meant I was competing against the very best people on television; actresses who'd been in the business for years, served their apprenticeships in the RSC and God knows where else, while I was just a jumped-up little nobody in a trashy soap opera. It was laughable, but really cool at the same time.

When I got to work that evening everyone seemed to have

heard already. If the other actors were pissed off they hid it well (skilful acting), and everyone talked about how good it was for the series and how it showed that the arts establishment was finally accepting that soaps were an art form. Everyone, including me, knew I didn't stand a chance of winning, but it would be great to be there anyway as a contender.

As soon as they had congratulated me they all asked the same question: 'What will you wear?'

Chapter Fifteen

I finally managed to get hold of my sister Jenny on her mobile. 'Hi,' I said. 'It's me.'

'Hi,' she said. 'Cool.'

'How is it at home?'

'Fucking terrible. You really did it this time.'

I was about to protest that I hadn't actually done anything apart from be born to the wrong woman, but decided it would be a waste of my breath. 'Is Mum OK?'

'My mum or your mum?' she taunted.

'Your mum,' I replied, willing to humour her. 'I can't get hold of her.'

'He smashed her phone, just before he smashed her and the rest of the house.'

'How was any of it her fault?'

'He was on the whisky, and angry.'

'I'd really like to see her, to talk to her.'

'He's away a few days next week, working up north or something. I think he's going on Monday.'

'Thanks.'

'No problem.'

She hung up as casually as if we had conversations like that several times a day. After work on Monday I hired a minicab, because it would be less conspicuous than a black cab, and headed back home. It felt odd to be back after so long, everything so familiar but strange at the same time. So much had happened to me since the last time I was there but I could still see the same faces on the streets and it didn't look as if anything had changed in their lives. No one gave me a second glance in the tatty-looking car. The driver was Asian and used to carrying actors from *The Towers*, so he left me alone with my thoughts all the way over. It was still light and there were kids playing outside as I got out, asking him to wait. I had no idea how long I was going to be, but I had his mobile number if I needed him. He didn't seem bothered. He knew where I worked; he could find me again if necessary. He settled down with the radio on and a creased Tom Clancy paperback.

Jenny obviously hadn't told Mum about my call because she looked genuinely startled to see me, tears springing to her eyes as she held out her arms and I fell into them.

'I'm so sorry, child,' she murmured, rubbing my back, 'so sorry.'

I was surprised again by how short she seemed, her head resting on my shoulder rather than the other way round, as I would have expected. I guess I hadn't really been looking at her before, when she was just my mum, someone who was always around when I was tiny and everyone seemed big. She bustled me through to the kitchen, wiping her eyes as she went. There was no one else in, which was a relief. I wanted it to be just her and me.

Once she'd made me a cup of tea and we'd sat down at the

table, she took my hand tightly in hers. 'I want you to know that you were always a daughter to me, child,' she said. 'I never thought of you as any different to the others, just because you didn't spring from my womb. You were a gift from God just as surely as any of them.'

'What happened?'

'Your father made a mistake, a bad mistake. He's not a bad man, but he can be a stupid one, as you know, when he's in the drink. He was in the drink the night you were conceived, but his stupidity turned out to be a blessing for us all.'

'A married man knocking up a stripper seems pretty fucking bad to me,' I said and the look of pain that shot across her face at my vulgarity made me feel guilty. 'How did I come to be with you, then?'

'It was the only way he could persuade her not to get rid of you.' She squeezed my fingers even harder as if to help me through the pain of this revelation, but having met Maggie it didn't come as a big surprise. 'He confessed to me as soon as he found out what he had done. He begged me to help him. She said that if we promised to look after you then she would go full term. Your father had to work a lot of overtime to compensate her for the months she couldn't work, but she stuck to her word. She wasn't such a bad woman as all that. She gave birth to you and then she let us have you.'

'Weren't you angry with Dad for betraying you?'

'Of course.' She laughed softly as if at a pleasant memory. 'I gave him hell for a few weeks and he had no choice but to take it. But you can't live like that forever, especially when you have been given a beautiful new life to care for. You were always a beautiful baby and I thanked God for the honour of being the one to bring you up.'

'Did she ever come to visit? To see how I was getting on?'

'No, I made her promise that she would stay away. I wanted you for my own. I didn't want to share you with her. Did I do wrong?'

'No, of course you didn't.'

The whole sanctimonious bit was beginning to get on my nerves, but I could hardly say anything when the woman had given up so much in order to love me.

'Have you met her?' she asked.

'Briefly. She's pretty rough trade.'

'She's your mother, child, you must be respectful.'

That was about as much sugar as I could take in one go, so I gave her a hug and left to find my taxi driver, promising to come back soon. I gave her a new mobile phone I'd bought and made her promise to keep it out of Dad's sight. At least now I could stay in touch with her again. Some of the local kids had gathered around the taxi by the time I got back there and the driver was looking nervous behind locked doors and tightly closed windows. He had given up even pretending to read his book and his eyes were rolling around all over the place. All credit to him for not just driving off and leaving me stranded.

'Hey, you're Steffi McBride,' one of the girls said as I walked through them and the crowd parted respectfully. I remembered her as being a lot younger.

'Hi, Tina,' I said. 'How's it going?'

'Usual shit. Nothing changes. You doing more music?'

'I don't know. I'm pretty busy.'

'You should do more music,' she said, snapping her fingers appreciatively. 'That telly stuff is crap. I've written some songs, you want to hear them?'

'Sure.'

I leaned back against the car and the driver, sensing he was now safe, opened his window to listen to Tina's rap. It wasn't bad. There are so many people out there with a bit of talent who just need a break. If I hadn't met Dora I would probably still have been in much the same place as these guys, just a few years older and a few years more disillusioned. Mind you, a group like this would have thought themselves way too cool to hang out with someone like me the way I was then, someone who actually quite liked school and didn't mind going to work in hotel kitchens.

'You want to text me those lyrics?' I asked, giving her my number. 'Maybe I can do something. No promises.'

'Promises are all bullshit,' she grinned. 'I remember when you lived round here. You were always an odd one.'

'She was the hot one,' one of the brothers added.

'How come you never told me that then?' I teased and he looked bashful, which blew his tough-guy act.

'You were with Pete,' he said. 'Pete had a lot of respect.'

'Anyone hear from him now?' I asked.

'He's around. They don't come looking for him so much now. You want to see him? I can take you to him.'

'Sure.' I felt a tremor of excitement at the thought of seeing Pete again. I had no idea what sort of reception I would get.

A couple of the kids climbed into the car with me, the one

in the front giving the driver instructions that took us down some streets even I had never been to before. Every house was boarded up, but they knew which boards to knock on to get a response. I waited in the car till Pete emerged, blinking in the light, and then climbed tentatively out.

He flashed a bright grin. 'Hey, the Queen of the World has come slumming.'

'Fuck off, Pete. You OK?'

'Sure, yeah.'

I could see he was tripping. It felt oddly nostalgic to be with him like that. I felt like tearing his clothes off and licking him all over, but I knew it was too late for that. He was right in a way: I was slumming and there was no way I could have gone through those boarded windows into the darkness beyond like I would have done a few months before. I wasn't part of that world any more and I felt a stab of sadness, because what had I replaced it with?

I was vaguely aware of a figure lurking in the background, but we had been talking for a few minutes before I realised he was filming. I guess I must have been tense anyway because this acted like a match to gunpowder and I went off like a rocket, screaming abuse. To his professional credit the guy kept the camera running as I charged towards him, even when I stabbed the toe of my boot into his shin and he started to crumple to the floor, the camera still pointing up at me, buzzing away, taking in the whole magnificence of my fury.

'What the fuck are you doing, man?' Pete asked, genuinely confused by my sudden burst of action.

'I'm sick to death of these bastards,' I screamed. 'They

follow me everywhere, poking their noses into every fucking corner of my life!'

'Wow, babe!' He put a steadying hand on my arm, pulling me back as I landed another kick. 'That's *my* film crew, man. They're making a documentary about me and my music.'

I couldn't believe it; the guy was still filming as he hauled himself back to his feet. He wasn't even moaning or anything and I know for sure it must have hurt like fuck because I put my full weight into that kick and they were mean boots.

'Ah, shit, Pete, you didn't say.'

He was laughing.

'It's not fucking funny, Pete, I could have killed him.'

I was trying to apologise to the guy, trying to explain that I'd never done anything like that before in my life, but the camera was still running and I could imagine how pathetic and ridiculous I was sounding, so I gave up and retreated to the safety of the taxi while Pete and his team slunk back into the building to continue being filmed. It was only once we were well away from the area that I realised exactly what had happened. They were making a film about Pete to promote his music? How the fuck did that happen? Last time I'd heard he was a fucking fugitive from justice.

By the time I got back home that night I felt more depressed than I had ever felt before – which was pretty weird, really, considering how well most things in my life were going. There was a photographer lurking in the street outside who fired off at least fifty shots of me between the car and the front door. I said hi to him but he didn't respond, just kept firing away. If he'd been halfway polite I might have invited him in

183

for a drink, just to have some company for a while and maybe to make up for kicking the shit out of the other poor guy. Missed an opportunity there, silly sod. Probably could have made another ten grand out of a few shots of me at home.

Once I was inside I wasn't sure what to do. I would have asked Gerry round, but I knew he was out working on a location shoot. I didn't fancy getting drunk on my own.

I scrolled back through my phone to a message Quentin James had left me a week or so before, with Maggie's address and number. I'd been pissed off when he sent it. I didn't think it was any of his business to try to act the cupid in our mother–daughter horror story. But I hadn't deleted it, so God knows what was going on in my subconscious. I thought about ringing to see if she was in but changed my mind. I slipped out the back door in case the photographer was still there, and went in search of another taxi.

Chapter Sixteen

The address was in Earl's Court, an area of west London I wasn't familiar with. It was a basement flat in an old red-brick building that must once have been quite grand, just behind the crowded, noisy main street. As I descended the steps into the damp shadow of the building a shiver ran right through me. It felt a bit like I was walking back into my own past, a time before I was even born. Very weird. I was tempted to turn and run and lose myself in the bustle and roar of the Earl's Court Road, even after I'd knocked on the door. I forced myself to stay put and wait to see what was going to happen next.

I could see someone approaching through the frosted glass, but it was still a shock when the door jerked open and I saw her face. She looked like something from a horror movie. She must have been wearing a wig at Quentin's office because her real hair was shorter and almost white. The hint of yellow could have been the last remnants of a blonde past, or could have been nicotine staining. But more shocking than that was the state of her face. It looked like she'd been caught in a house fire, all the skin burned and sore, plasters everywhere. She was wearing dark glasses despite the fact that it was evening and the flat behind her was dimly lit.

'Hi,' I said, trying to recover my composure. 'It's Steffi.'

'Christ,' she said. 'You'd better come in.'

She stood back to let me in. The smell of smoke and stale cooking was overpowering. The place was quite tidy and clean, but shabby, like nothing had been replaced or repaired or decorated in twenty years. She led me into a small sitting room next to the front door. There were bars over the window to deter intruders and a gas fire, which had added another smell to the stale air. There were photographs everywhere, most of them of her, some obviously studio portraits taken to try to get modelling or acting work, others snaps taken with people who had the look of celebrities, although I didn't recognise any of them. It was shocking how much I looked like her when she was younger, except that she had dark hair and eyebrows, not like I'd imagined at all. It was like seeing myself dressed up for a part set in the 1970s or 1980s.

'If I'd known you were coming I could have warned you,' she said, gesturing at her face.

'What happened?'

She laughed. 'Nothing happened. Self-inflicted. Finest plastic surgeon in Harley Street, or so he tells me. I'm having a make-over. It's part of Quentin's plan to relaunch my career.'

'A televised facelift?'

'When I did the story I told him I needed enough money for a facelift and he said he could do better than that – said he could arrange for a documentary, which would mean I would get paid and they would pay all the expenses; plus I get the exposure on prime-time telly.'

It all sounded a bit desperate to me, but I didn't say anything.

'Hope it's all right of me to pop in like this.'

'Of course. I hoped you would.'

She didn't ask me how I knew the address, so I guessed she must have known about Quentin texting me.

'Do you want a drink?' she asked.

The business of fetching ice and cutting slices of lemon filled the next few awkward minutes.

'Has Quentin got any other plans for you, then?' I asked, as the atmosphere became a little more comfortable.

'Plenty. Listen, I know it looks like I'm cashing in on your success …'

I said nothing.

'But you can see that things are pretty desperate. I don't have many more chances to make it.'

'He seems a bit of a sleazeball to me,' I said.

'I've met worse.' She shrugged. 'Hell, I've gone out with worse. Quentin and me, we go back a long way together. More than once he's helped me raise money when it looked like I was just about to go under.'

'You've sold stories through him before?'

'Quentin knows where all the skeletons are hidden.' She gave a throaty smoker's laugh.

It seemed odd to think that a man like Quentin knew things about my past that I didn't, like he was some spooky, all-knowing, behind-the-scenes manipulator – which, I guess, is exactly what he is.

'How did you meet Dad?' I asked. I'd read most of the story in the papers by then, but I needed something to talk about, and my experience had taught me that reporters didn't always tell the whole story.

She took a long drink. 'I was working in a place called Raymond's Revue Bar. It was the best strip joint in London, probably in Europe, at the time – world famous. Big shows with costumes and proper choreography. Sometimes Raymond would introduce us to the punters after the show. Nothing was expected, unless you wanted to arrange it yourself. Your dad was there with a stag party. They were bloody drunk, but he was a good-looking guy and we sort of clicked.'

'Did he tell you he was married?'

'Not the sort of thing that would come up in conversation at a place like that.'

'No, I suppose not.' I knew I was in danger of coming across like someone's disapproving maiden aunt.

'Anyway, there was a chemistry and we got it together. He took precautions, but it must have ripped.'

That was more information than I needed, but I said nothing, taking a large swallow of gin while I absorbed the story so far.

'Where did you go?' I asked, not sure why I felt the need to know. 'A hotel?'

'Good God, no,' she laughed again. 'Neither of us could have afforded a hotel. He came back here.'

That was a shock. I was actually sitting in the flat where I had been conceived. She had been living in this hole for all those years; that was depressing.

'So, it was just a one-night stand?'

'Not exactly, but once he discovered I was pregnant he got

all pious and Catholic on me. I would have had an abortion if he'd been willing to pay. Sorry,' she said with a grimace, 'but I would. He said that would be a sin, gave me the whole spiel; said he would bring you up himself. I didn't think he was serious, I certainly didn't think his wife would agree. When she did it seemed like the perfect answer.'

'And they paid you?'

'I had to live and I needed to stay healthy till you were born. Not a big demand for pregnant strippers.'

We sat in silence for a few minutes. It was a bit of a slap in the face to know your own mother would have got rid of you if she'd had her way, but the thought that Dad had wanted me so much he was actually willing to go to Mum and confess all made me feel quite tearful in a good way. He might be a moody, stubborn, violent old bastard who couldn't hold his drink, but at least he'd wanted me. Mum must have wanted me too, otherwise she wouldn't have been willing to treat me like one of hers for all those years. It's funny the places where you can find a bit of consolation for life's tougher blows, isn't it?

'How old was I when you handed me over?'

'They took you away immediately. I never even saw you. All I knew was that you were a girl.'

'And you never wanted to get in touch, find out how I was doing?'

'Sometimes.' She shrugged. 'But I'd made a deal, promised not to. I even came over and sat outside your block once or twice, hoping to catch a glimpse of you, but you never came out while I was there. I sort of felt sure I would recognise you if you did. I was pretty busy after that, getting my career going again.'

Another silence fell as I tried to work out what I was feeling.

'I read in *The Stage* that you're nominated for a Bafta,' she filled the silence. 'That's a hell of a good break.'

'Yeah, thanks. There's no chance I'll get it. They must have been short of people to nominate this year.'

'Don't put yourself down, you're a talented actress. It's in your genes.'

'Thanks,' I said again, although I knew she was complimenting herself as much as me.

'What will you wear?'

'I don't know. Everyone asks that.'

'All the designers will be on to you, wanting to lend you stuff.'

'Yeah, my agent has told me. I'm not really into all that. I like vintage. I'll probably pick up something in Camden Market.'

'You like vintage?'

'Well, Oxfam mostly.'

'Ever heard of a 1970s designer called Bill Gibb?'

'No.'

'Same period as Zandra Rhodes and that lot, but he died early. His stuff was always in *Vogue*; magical, beautiful designs. I modelled for him once.'

'Yeah?'

'At the Albert Hall. It was this huge charity production.'

Just remembering her glory days was making her sit up straighter, raising her chin and running her fingers through her sparse hair as if it were still beautiful.

'I was dating this guy who was one of Bill's backers. He

Caroline
20th

Tony
23rd.

gave me one of Bill's originals, had it made to measure, real couture perfection. Everyone modelling that day was wearing their own Bill Gibb originals; all the most beautiful actresses and models and society girls. Everyone loved Bill, they were all happy to do it for him. It was a fabulous night.'

'Pity you don't still have it,' I joked.

'I do. Do you want to see it?'

'That would be great.' It was a relief to find something neutral to talk about.

She led me through into the bedroom, which was even darker than the sitting room. The unmade bed was a tousled mess of dark-red and black bedclothes; there were more pictures of her on the walls. In the corner of the room was a wicker peacock chair covered in leopardskin-print cushions. She saw me looking at it.

'Biba. The whole flat was Biba once, but things get broken and wear out. There's never been anything like it since.'

The air was clearer in there, as if she had a no-smoking rule in there at least. An ancient dark-wood wardrobe dominated one side of the room, covered in hangers and clothes. She lifted them off, throwing them on to the bed, so she could open one of the doors. Inside the rail was crowded but she seemed to know exactly what she was looking for and pulled out a dress in a plastic cover. She threw it on to the bed on top of everything else and directed the bedside light at it, as if arranging a spotlight on a stage, before unzipping the bag and lovingly lifting the gown free. I had been all set to make some polite comments but I actually gasped at the beauty of the gown that emerged. It had been stitched together with

191

intricate layers of feathers and beads on a background of lace and silk. It was the sort of dress a little girl might imagine a fairy princess to wear. It was a fantasy.

'It was the one that the press liked,' she said wistfully. 'We were on the front of all the papers the following day; even Twiggy didn't get as many column inches. I'll show you the cuttings.'

'It's beautiful,' I whispered, gently stroking the feathers as if they were still attached to a living creature. It seemed incredible that an object of such beauty and delicacy could be living in such a terrible, sad, shabby place, imprisoned in the dark when it should be out in the spotlight.

'Do you want to try it on? You look about the same size I was then.'

'Oh, I don't know.' I wasn't sure I was quite ready for such an intimate moment with Maggie.

'Go on,' she coaxed. 'I dare you!'

I giggled stupidly, excitedly, like we were naughty schoolgirls raiding a grown-up wardrobe together. 'OK.'

She helped me into it and it felt as wonderful as it looked. She must have been exactly the same size as me when she was my age because it fitted perfectly, like Cinderella's slipper.

'You should wear it to the Baftas,' she said. 'That way at least you'll get the press coverage, even if you don't get the award.'

Chapter Seventeen

Once the news got out that I was up for an award all the big London designers contacted me, trying to tempt me to wear one of their dresses. I went to see them all because it was such a laugh. It was like being a little girl with the biggest dressing-up cupboard in the world, but I didn't like many of the frocks they tried to talk me into. What surprised me was how grown up some of them made me look. I didn't think I was ready to look like that yet. I would have felt like a fraud swanning up the red carpet in some slinky Valentino or Chanel number. But that didn't mean I didn't enjoy all the attention I got from their public relations people, all the champagne they plied me with while incredibly posh people rushed around suggesting jewellery I should borrow and shoes I should try.

It was like they were all looking at me and none of them could see that I was just a south-London girl who'd got lucky. Through their rose-tinted shades they seemed to be seeing someone like Grace Kelly or Audrey Hepburn, while I still felt like Steffi from the squat.

None of the things they showed me was a patch on Maggie's dress. By the end of our evening together I had actually felt quite fond of her. I mean, I didn't want to think too hard about the state of her maternal instincts or her morals, but as a friend I thought she might turn out to be a bit of a laugh. As a gesture I said I would be happy to be filmed for her make-over documentary if she thought it would help to pull in a few more viewers. It seemed to me she was going through an awful lot of agony just for one more shot at the big time, so maybe she deserved a bit of support, especially as it was no skin off my nose (no pun intended there).

Quentin rang me the next day to see if I had been serious about the offer. Now that I knew he was an old friend of Maggie's I felt a bit of an obligation to be nice to him, like I might be to a lechy old uncle at a wedding. It was set up for me to come along to see her once the transformation was done, so they could film my reaction.

'I've got a lot of plans for your mother,' he said. It sounded funny to have her referred to like she was a big part of my life, but I let it pass. 'And your friend Pete.'

'Pete?'

'We're getting together a record deal for him. He's very talented.'

'You're behind that?'

'Absolutely. I told you no one escapes me for long.'

I had mixed feelings about that. It did seem like he was snooping around every part of my life, but at the same time I was happy to think that Pete might be getting his big break because of me. I felt that made up a bit for me messing him around with Luke.

After the first visit to Maggie's I found myself thinking about her a lot, and thinking about her led to me getting back in a taxi again a few evenings later. This time I went armed with flowers and was shocked to see her eyes watering up when I gave them to her. I guess it had probably been a while. She had her wig on, which made her look less shocking, and the plasters were coming off, although her skin still looked terribly raw. She had lost the dark glasses and her eyes had scars all round them where the surgeon had removed the loose skin. She'd just spent the day at the dentist having major stuff done to her teeth and the immaculate white results looked a bit shocking, like a brand-new Bentley parked in the middle of bombsite.

'I've got to do it, haven't I?' she said once we were sitting down with the gin bottle.

'Do what?'

'Give up smoking. I can't put myself through all of this and then turn everything yellow again, can I?'

'Might be a bit of a waste.'

Not knowing what to do with her hands without a constant supply of cigarettes, she took too many nervous sips at her glass and was having to refill it while I was still only halfway down mine.

'Were you ever married?' I asked.

'Came close a few times, in the early days, when rich men were still taking an interest. I worked at a casino in the West End as a croupier and had a couple of interesting proposals there.'

'Why didn't you, then?'

She narrowed her eyes and stared at me and for a moment I thought she was going to tell me to mind my own business. 'Couldn't imagine giving up my ambitions. What man would be willing to put up with a woman hustling her way up through the show-business jungle? If I'd married I would've had to admit defeat on all that; give up my dream.'

We both fell silent at that, me thinking about the fact that I'd given up Luke and her probably thinking about a lot more than that.

'Can you understand that?' she asked eventually.

'Oh, yes.'

'Not many women can. Most of them, by the time they get to my age, think I've made all the wrong choices. They look at this –' she gestured round the room '– and they compare it to their big houses and their family holidays and their big fat pensions, and they think I'm deluded. But they've never known what it feels like to be standing in a spotlight with every pair of eyes in the room on you as you dance or sing or whatever. Or, if they have, they've forgotten it. They've forgotten what it feels like to be the centre of attention. Would I rather be spending my days cooking meals, doing school runs and going to coffee mornings?'

She left the question unanswered and I waited for her to go on.

'I know I haven't made it yet, but I still could. Every day that I wake up there's a chance that something amazing will happen; a hit record or a television job, something that will be the big break I need to get back on top.'

'Did you act, then?'

'Still do when I can get the jobs. It's usually background work but sometimes I get a line and you never know, do you? I played a patient in *Casualty* a year or so ago, but they made me up to be dying of cancer so you'd never have known. If this make-over programme does OK it could lead to something else. Maybe I could end up as your neighbour at *The Towers*.'

I laughed politely, but I actually felt a tremor of anxiety, like she was threatening my private territory. I was happy to spend time with her as long as it was here, in her dingy basement, which I could escape from at any time. I wasn't sure how I would feel about having her in my life any more than that. I was shocked by my readiness to reject her as quickly as she had once rejected me. She topped up my glass. If she had seen the horror on my face she didn't mention it.

'What other stories has Quentin sold for you in the past?' I asked.

'Kiss and tell, you know the sort of thing. I hung out with the pop groups in the 1970s, and with a few footballers later on. There was a politician once. The media loves all that. Stories about Christine Keeler and Mandy Rice-Davies; names that won't mean much to you now but were big in their time.'

'Didn't you feel guilty about grassing on your lovers?'

'They always benefited in the end – raised their profiles in the media, came out looking like super-studs.'

'What about their marriages?'

'If they were screwing girls like me on the side their marriages were pretty fucked anyway, don't you think? Some girls I knew would encourage their lovers to get divorces and marry them, and then take them to the cleaners later. At least I never did that.'

'Most people end up getting married and then staying together, though, don't they?'

She nodded. 'Yes. But then most people give up on their dreams quite quickly, maybe before they've even left school. I never wanted to do that.'

'How do you know that your dreams aren't just fantasies?'

'Well, you don't, until they come true. But having fantasies can be fun too. I'm not sure most people's reality is that great.'

It felt like I was talking to a real-life, older version of Nikki. Maggie was a one-woman research project for an aspiring young actress.

'What about you?' she changed the subject. 'What was the story behind the boy with the gun?'

'Pete? He was my first love, childhood sweetheart, but he got too much into the drugs, frazzled his brain. He was sweet, though.'

'Yeah, but a gun. Fucking hell, Steff …'

'I know, but it's all calmed down now. Quentin's trying to get him a music career.'

She laughed. 'That man never misses a trick. With Quentin behind him it just might happen. And what about the pop singer?'

'Luke? I've been in love with him since I was 12.' I grinned sheepishly.

'Ah, so you have fantasies too. Or is it a dream come true?'

I shrugged, not wanting to let her into that part of my life – not yet, anyway. It was still all much too raw and painful. I changed the subject.

'Did you mean it when you said I could wear your dress for the Baftas?'

Chapter Eighteen

I have to admit, the day of the Baftas was a bit of a buzz. They really know how to make you feel like a star. Cars appear magically to ferry you around and an army of hairdressers, make-up artists and stylists are put at your disposal. But by the time we got that far I had a pretty good idea of how I wanted to look. This was like standing in front of Mum's bedroom mirror with the dressing-up clothes – times about five million. Having decided on using Maggie's dress, confident that no one else would have anything like it, I was going to go for a fairly stripped-down look in the face department, but with lashings of eyeliner and mascara; sort of Romany version of Twiggy meets Dusty Springfield and Amy Winehouse, if you get what I mean.

Gerry said he thought it was a good idea, although he probably would have said that if I'd suggested going as a sack of King Edwards. He'd found himself a tuxedo in the Oxfam shop, which he was teaming up with his best pair of trainers (even I thought his favourite desert boots would not be appropriate, as much due to the stink they gave off as anything else). Our main problem was keeping his shirt tucked into the rather slack waistband of the trousers, but in the end I gave up even bothering to mention it and concentrated on trying to bring his hair under control.

'Your mum'll be watching this,' I reminded him. 'You want to make her proud, don't you?'

He didn't disagree, but he didn't exactly help either. It was lovely to have his soothing presence there beside me and I forced myself not to think about how much more lovely it would be if it was Luke. I hadn't heard anything from him since the split and I didn't contact him either, not wanting him to think I was going to be one of those girls who had trouble letting go. There were moments when I thought I was being pathetic and endangering my whole future happiness just by being too proud to beg him to have another go. But then I would decide it would be more pathetic to be clinging on if he really wasn't going to be able to hack me having a career. Back and forth, back and forth, feeling guilty all the time about even thinking such thoughts when Gerry was around and being so totally sweet. Why does life have to be so fucking complicated all the time?

I could see as the day progressed that some of the professionals in the styling department were a bit doubtful about the dress. I dare say they gave Diane Keaton the same sort of looks the year she went to the Oscars dressed as Charlie Chaplin, and I'm sure there were people who told Cher she was overdoing it when she wore that spider's web of a frock to accept her Oscar – but which are the outfits that stick in the memory? As you can see, I have made a bit of a study of these sorts of things, never happier than when settled down in front of an awards ceremony practising my own imaginary acceptance speeches. The funny thing was that, now I was actually nominated, I no longer had a prepared speech. I'm not sure if that was because I truly didn't believe I had a chance or for some deeply superstitious reason.

Walking down the red carpet towards the Palladium was really wicked. I'd been down a few before, premieres and that sort of thing, but this was different. This was the big time; lines of security men holding back the banks of media, flaming torches to light our way, limos timed to arrive at exactly the right moment, the whole mini-Oscar experience. Lush. As our car drew up at the end of the carpet and I saw some of the other dresses ahead, I had a momentary frisson of terror that I might have made a terrible mistake – was it possible to be *too* different and to stand out *too* much? But by then it was too late. The car door opened and I stepped out, with Gerry shambling behind, his hair looking like it could give Russell Brand a run for his money.

As we progressed, the weirdest thing seemed to happen. The cheering grew louder and the barriers seemed to sag towards us. Police and security guards who had been standing around like waxworks suddenly sprang into action, trying to hold people back. I couldn't work out what was going on. Cameras were going off and a platoon of microphones was charging towards us:

'Steffi!'

'Nikki!'

'Over here, Steff!'

'Where's Luke?'

'Where's your mum?'

'How's Maggie?'

'Any sign of Pete?'

'Who's the bloke with you?'

It was like a scene from *The Day of the Locust*. (It's a good movie, if you're into the whole Hollywood Dream thing. Gerry had introduced me to the book and then searched out the DVD to distract me one evening when I was feeling low. Gerry has studied the camera angles of virtually every film ever made.) For a moment I felt a genuine fear that we were going to be trampled underfoot. It became confusing as more police rushed forward and Gerry put his arms around me as we ran together towards the entrance, other celebrities scattering in our wake. There was no chance of stopping to answer any of the questions.

As we got to the Palladium steps another line of security men assembled between us and the crowd and I turned to give them all a wave. I didn't want people to think I was becoming all snotty and starry and wasn't willing to be friendly. The flashing of cameras was almost blinding as the police moved the paparazzi back behind the hastily reassembled barriers and the management of the event ushered us inside. Although the officials all looked anxious and unsettled, it was obvious they were enjoying the excitement. A scene like this would ensure the awards went to the top of every news bulletin that night; they just didn't want it to be because there had been any injuries. Getting on the news meant more exposure for the programmes being honoured, which would inevitably lead to more bums on seats and advertising sales; cash registers ringing all round.

There were more photographers and reporters inside, the

honoured ones, and hordes of friendly faces from *The Towers* and rival soaps, as well as some even more famous television faces. People were talking to one another about the loss of crowd control outside, as if we had all just been through the Blitz together. Everyone was very sweet about the dress, although I suspect most of the women were more impressed I had the nerve to wear something so outlandish than they were with the actual history of the design. Gerry was the perfect consort, staying a couple of paces behind, grinning amiably at the few people who bothered to look in his direction. It would have annoyed me – the way everyone showed no interest in him because he was 'just' a cameraman – if I hadn't been so sure he was totally unbothered. Luke might not have been able to handle the thought of being in my shadow at these sorts of events, but Gerry obviously thrived there like a cheerful sort of mushroom.

Once we were inside the auditorium there were other members of the production team for Gerry to talk to until it was time for us all to settle in our seats. The atmosphere was a bit like a cross between the last day of a school term and a works outing. Other people's partners were looking a bit left out while everyone else talked shop, discussing the people in the running for all the different awards, giggling and bitching. Everyone inside had heard about the crowds breaking through the barriers, but no one seemed to have connected it to the moment when we arrived. Now that it was over, I wasn't even sure that it had had anything to do with us. Maybe it had just been a coincidence; after all, why would the crowd behave any differently for me and Gerry?

It has to be said, live awards shows are pretty boring unless they're about you or people you know. The bits you see on telly are really just the highlights. For every recognisable face there are about ten men in dinner suits accepting awards for something technical. Not that I'm dissing the production guys, they are just as important as the actors – more important, actually – but watching them collect awards isn't so great. After what seemed like an age, we got to the acting ones and as the moment for 'actress of the year' drew closer I felt my stomach tightening. I told myself it was ridiculous because I didn't have a chance of winning, but just the thought that I might pull a bad face at the moment of losing was making me want to shit myself. What is the best face to pull when the camera turns on you two seconds after you've learned that someone else has got your award? Fixed smile is probably the best, and lots of enthusiastic clapping. So I was bracing myself for that when I heard the words.

'And the winner is … Steffi McBride.'

For a few seconds I couldn't make sense of it; I couldn't remember what a winner was supposed to do, where I was supposed to go, what I was supposed to say. All those years of practising thank-you speeches in Mum's bedroom mirror abandoned me and I was left with an empty void where my brain had once been. Helpful hands in the seats around lifted me to my feet and propelled me to the end of the row. Gerry gave me a huge hug, which practically knocked me back down off my feet again. He then stayed standing to cheer and whoop and wave his arms in the air as I stumbled down the aisle and was helped up on to the stage. Suddenly the world was reversed and the place where I had been sitting, almost anonymously, was suddenly a huge sea of faces, all staring up at me. Someone was shaking my hand, someone was kissing me, lights were in my eyes, music was blaring and then dying away, I had an award in my hands, I was standing at the podium and suddenly there was silence as they waited to hear what I had to say. I had nothing to say. I racked my brain for what seemed like hours but was probably just a few seconds. Nothing clever or witty came to me.

'I would like to thank my mum and dad,' I said, feeling the tears prickle up and my throat constrict. 'And my brothers and sisters, and Dora and Gerry and Luke and everyone at *The Towers* who made me feel so welcome.'

I paused for breath and the music started again. Thank God. More helpful hands guided me back down off the stage as the cameras moved on to the next announcer and the next potential recipients. I hurried back to my seat and the comfort of Gerry's arm as I snuggled in close to him and stared hard at the stage, as if I was taking in what was happening to anyone else at that moment, waiting for my heart to stop thumping quite so fast.

After the show a group of us went down to Joe Allen's in Covent Garden for a meal. It was like one huge party, with everyone coming up to me, offering congratulations and saying how much they liked the dress (my main worry was getting relish from my burger down it). Someone had a mobile television, which showed the evening news with the crowds breaking through the barriers and then film of me accepting the award. It was obvious from the news clips that the incident had been triggered by the media all surging towards Gerry and me at once, pressured by the people behind them who were trying to take a look. The dress looked great on the cameras, although I thought my make-up made me look a bit like a startled panda bear, but that was OK – quite a sexy look, really.

By the time we stumbled out of Joe Allen's the morning papers were hitting the streets and someone found us a complete set. I was on the front page of every single one, even the *Financial Times*. The tabloids had majored in on Gerry, 'the new man in my life', and one or two of them had found pictures of Luke looking sad and alone in their files and printed them alongside the Bafta shots, giving the impression that he was broken-hearted. Bastards!

The producers had booked a suite at the Savoy and we all staggered over there for more cocktails and were still there when it was time for breakfast. It was just like being in the movies, a dream sequence. By the time Gerry and I got home I was buzzing from a mixture of excitement, caffeine and exhaustion. There was another crowd of photographers waiting outside the house, hoping to see me falling over drunk, probably, but I managed to disappoint them on that one, compensating with a cheery wave of the award.

'Over here, Gerry!'

'Give her a hug, Gerry!'

'A kiss for the cameras!'

'How long have you been together?'

'Any chance of wedding bells?'

We closed the door on them.

'How much longer do you think you can go on living here?' Gerry asked, slumping on to the sofa. 'If you're going to become a mega-star you are going to need somewhere a bit more secure than this. You'll also need to invest all the money that's going to come pouring in.'

'It won't last,' I said, kicking off my shoes and lying down beside him. 'It'll be someone else's turn next year and they will all have moved to another doorstep. It's not a problem.'

'You still need to talk to Dora about it.'

The night seemed unfinished in some way, as if there was a gap, something I needed to do. I realised that I wanted to make my peace with Dad. I knew he would be up by now, and he would have seen a paper because that was always the first thing he did in the morning. He would probably have caught the television news before leaving home as well. I dialled his mobile number for the first time since leaving home. I knew there was a chance he wouldn't pick up when he saw it was me, but there was also a chance he would have removed my number from his address book the day he decided to have no more to do with me, and so wouldn't know who was calling.

'Yes?' he answered and my heart jumped.

'Hi, Dad, it's Steffi. How are you?'

'What do you want?'

'I just wanted to say hi, and maybe arrange to come round and see you. What do you think?'

'I think you've got the fancy life you always wanted now. You don't need to be bothering us for anything again. Just leave us all alone.'

The line went dead.

Chapter Nineteen

Dora agreed with Gerry about the house. 'I'd been thinking the same thing myself,' she said when I mentioned it. 'You need somewhere more secure. You probably need to be in the country.'

'I'm not really a country person,' I said doubtfully.

My only experience so far had been with Luke's family, but I couldn't actually imagine living like that on my own. Even though they had been in the country they had been like a little community themselves, not stuck out all alone in the middle of nowhere.

'Well, maybe not the real country,' she said. 'A nice suburban house in its own grounds would be good. I'll work out what you can afford and come up with a few places for you to see. There are people who specialise in finding houses for celebrities. They know all about security.'

'Jesus, Dora, are you sure I need all that?'

'You saw what happened at the Baftas,' she said. 'Things get out of control very easily. And last time it was just Pete waving a gun about. Next time it might be a real nutter.'

'Are you deliberately trying to freak me out?'

'No,' she laughed. 'Of course not. But you've got to start

thinking about these things. And anyway, you want to be able to keep the photographers out a bit.'

Dad's words – 'You've got the fancy life you always wanted now' – kept echoing around in my head. I didn't want people thinking I was putting on airs and graces, pretending I was some sort of Lady of the Manor or something. All that had happened was I'd got a job in a soap opera and released a gimmicky pop record, I hadn't married the Prince of fucking Wales.

Dora wasn't letting the grass grow on this one and the next weekend she arranged for this poncey estate agent to pick Gerry and me up in his shiny BMW and cart us off around a few properties in Surrey. I have to say, it did not feel right. I was a bit nervous about Gerry at this stage; it was nice to have him there for company, but I didn't want him getting the idea that we were settling down as a couple because I was pretty sure he was not the man I was going to be spending the rest of my life with. The fact that pictures of Luke would come into my mind whenever Gerry and I had sex was a pretty good clue in that department. Not that there weren't moments when the thought of settling down comfortably with a man who was easily my best friend didn't hold a lot of appeal. Should I, I would wonder in moments of self-doubt, be grateful for what I was being offered and stop wishing for the impossible? How does that song go? Something about how if you can't be with the one you love, then you should love the one you are with. Was I in danger of ending up sad and alone like Maggie?

I was a bit shocked when Dora told me I had a million and a half to spend. 'A million and a half?' I shouted. 'That's a fucking fortune!'

'I got you a good deal on "Summer Wine",' she said modestly. 'And the advertising deals have been mounting up. On the strength of your Bafta-night triumph I can rope *OK!* in for at least another quarter of a million if they get first photographic rights, maybe even double that. And you can get a good mortgage against your salary now. It would be better to have the money in bricks and mortar. If we invest it in anything else you end up paying tax on the interest ...'

'Stop!' I held up my hand. 'You're doing my head in. Just tell me what to do.'

'Go buy a house.'

I was even more shocked, however, when the estate agent, who was called Nigel or something, told me, 'A million and a half doesn't buy you much in this area.'

'You should see the area I come from, mate,' I said and from then on he obviously had me down as being a bit chippy, which I suppose I was. Don't get me wrong: they were very nice houses. If I'd been planning to move in with a husband and Land Rover and four kids, and buy some ponies and maybe a Labrador or two, they would have been very suitable. But it was hard to see what one woman was going to do with three or four 'ensuite' bathrooms and God knows how many 'integral' garages. We saw glittering kitchens, gleaming bathrooms, laundry rooms and linen cupboards until our heads span. We enjoyed 'panoramic views' over 'sweeping lawns' and crunched across a lot of weedless gravel. One of them even had a 'gift-wrapping room'. I was beginning to feel deeply nostalgic for the squat with its dark and seedy cosiness.

The estate agent made a point of showing us how high the

walls were, how electric the gates were and how many different parts of the grounds could be watched through cameras. There was no chance poor old Pete was going to be able to sneak in unobserved to any of these places. I could see Gerry was getting as depressed as I was at the whole thing.

'If I move to one of those places I'll feel completely isolated from everyday life,' I moaned once we were back home. 'It would be like being marooned on a luxurious desert island. I'd be drinking myself to death within a week.'

'Welcome to leafy Celebsville,' Gerry said, with a grin.

The next day the papers were full of stories about how Gerry and I were house hunting together for a 'love nest'. Nigel, or whatever his name was, must have snitched on us two seconds after waving goodbye. Gerry pretended not to notice the stories and so I didn't say anything, but it was bloody embarrassing.

'I think it might be better to buy a flat in London for the moment,' I told Dora. 'I don't think I'm ready to be quite that grown up.'

'OK. There's lots of good investment properties in Docklands. Fancy that?'

The next weekend we were escorted round a succession of river views in converted warehouses and I was so grateful not to be moving to Surrey that I just plumped for a pimped-up penthouse where one of the bedrooms had been converted into a little private cinema. Dora had bought it for me by the end of the week.

My first night there was pretty much ruined by someone giving me a copy of *Hello!* with a photo spread of Luke and some bimbo model I'd never heard of. So much for him pining away without me, the bastard! They were draped all over each other in some swanky country house hotel and I was shocked by just how acute the pain was as I looked at them. I wasn't sure how I was going to be able to cope if I went on feeling like that for much longer. At the same time a nasty little voice in my head was nagging away that I was just kidding myself, Luke had moved on and it was pointless holding on to any fantasies about him turning up on the doorstep and begging for a second chance.

I rang Gerry and told him I wasn't feeling well so wanted to be alone, and then sat up late in my new posh penthouse, drinking red wine and smoking a joint, watching the lights reflecting on the water, playing Roberta Flack through the perfect sound system and feeling really sorry for myself. Pretty pathetic, eh?

Once Quentin heard that I'd offered to take part in Maggie's make-over documentary he couldn't do enough to help and a few weeks later I found myself being whisked off to a boutique hotel in Kensington. I seemed to spend a large part of my life staring at the backs of drivers' necks, being whisked from one place to another. I thought it might be a good idea to learn to drive, but when would I find the time? And how vulnerable would I feel in a car on my own? Supposing I had a scrape or something in a busy street and had to get out and swap addresses? Imagine how embarrassing that would be. I never want to complain about being famous, but sometimes it would be nice just to do the same things as everyone else.

I was ushered into a suite by a really hyper presenter, under the all-too-familiar, silent gaze of a camera. It was the first show of the series and this girl was obviously hoping it was going to make her reputation, turn her into the new Davina McCall or Fearne Cotton or something. Turned out she was another of Quentin's clients. Surprise, surprise!

Back under the scrutiny of the camera, I found myself getting infected with her excitement and actually felt quite nervous about the impending meeting as they built up the tension. Whatever was filmed in this hotel suite was going to be presented to the watching world as my reunion with the mother who had abandoned me at birth. I would have felt a lot better if I'd had a scriptwriter and a director on hand to help me through the scene. What if I got it wrong and came across as bitter and twisted? What if Maggie got it wrong and came across as a cold-hearted bitch? Quentin had assured me I didn't need to worry, that he would be able to veto anything I didn't like before it went out, but I didn't trust him an inch. His job was to create as big a media stir as possible for Maggie and to get as many people as possible watching the show. I did some deep breathing to try to slow down my racing heart, but it wasn't working.

The presenter was really throwing her all into building the suspense for the great unveiling of their masterpiece and most of what she was saying was flying past me as I grinned and mugged inanely for the camera. Then the door to the bedroom opened and Maggie made her entrance.

Actually, I hardly had to fake my reaction at all, because she really did look stunning. Her face had healed and a make-up artist had done a brilliant job of making her look ten years younger. The teeth now looked like they belonged and someone had done something amazing with her hair, taking it back to blonde and cutting it into a fluffy, boyish style. They had dressed her in a silk top and narrow jeans that showed off her legs and the effect was pretty stunning. She looked very apprehensive and I genuinely wanted to reassure her as I put my arms around her. It didn't feel like being with my mother, but I did feel a strange surge of affection for her. I actually felt happy for her that she looked so great. That was the moment we both lost control. I think she started crying first, and her tears set me off. I must have been bottling up a lot of stuff, and Christ knows how many emotional boxes she'd stacked away in her life, because we both really let rip. It was television gold.

There was so much sobbing going on, the presenter actually forgot to stay upbeat and joined in the group hug. I was so moved and absorbed in what was going on between us I didn't notice the photographer moving carefully around behind the cameraman.

I have to say, Quentin James may be some kind of slimeball, but he sure knows how to gauge the mood of the public and milk it for all its worth. By the end of the day, 'stolen' snatches of the film were up on the Internet and being talked about on every sofa in every television studio in the land. The photographs of the reunion swamped the tabloids and magazines. The show was guaranteed a big audience and Maggie had got her showcase for the big time.

Whereas the media had been pretty vile and judgemental towards her up till then, angry with her for dumping her baby, they now suddenly changed their tack. I suppose they thought that, if I could forgive her, so should they. She was the prodigal mother returning to the fold, giving them endless amounts of material to write and moralise about – and they did.

But Quentin had one more trick up his sleeve. As a final scene for the programme he had arranged for her to perform some songs at Madame Jo-Jo's, a sometime gay and drag club just round the corner from Raymond's Revue Bar in Soho, where she had met Dad. He filled the place with celebrities and music-business contacts and asked me to go along. Gerry thought it would be a laugh and agreed to come with me. I have to say, they did Maggie proud. The lights were low, there was champagne on the tables and it was all very Marlene Dietrich and *Cabaret*. Maggie swished out in a really slinky Gucci dress and I actually felt the hairs rising on the back of my neck. Once in the spotlight, the old girl really did have some charisma. She did a few standards like Carly Simon's 'You're So Vain' and Peter Sarstedt's 'Where Do You Go To My Lovely?'. Then she finished with that Elkie Brooks song 'Pearl's A Singer'. Pearl was a nightclub singer doomed never to make the big time, but still clinging to dreams of a stardom that will never materialise. It seemed to evoke exactly what Maggie's life must have been like. She delivered it perfectly.

I looked around the room as she growled through the song with her smoky, gin-soaked voice and everyone was staring, rapt, not wanting to miss a second. For that moment she was a star. I knew she was completely content, because we had talked about moments like that, moments when everyone is watching you, listening to you, taking notice of you, loving you. Moments that can never last for long.

Chapter Twenty

'Does Luke have a grandfather called Robert?' Dora asked one morning as we had coffee in the penthouse and my heart missed a beat just at the sound of Luke's name. Was it ever going to stop doing that?

'Possibly. He has a grandfather, but everyone called him Grandpa when I was there.'

'Well, he sent you an email, care of me.'

'Grandpa did?'

I took the email from her and read it. It was an invitation to lunch from 'Robert Lewis (Luke's granddad)'.

'Posh lunch venue,' Dora said as I read it. 'Old-fashioned gentleman's club, better wear a frock. Want me to accept for you?'

'Sure, why not?'

Now my heart was really thumping, like I'd drunk six espressos on the trot. It was great to hear from the old boy, because I had liked him a lot, but it was really great to hear from anyone who had anything to do with Luke. I had tried as hard as I knew how to put him out of my mind. Gerry was so sweet to me, and such a good man, but I just couldn't shake Luke out of my thoughts. Hearing from his grandpa felt like hearing from my own family, like a call from home.

The taxi driver who dropped me off at Grandpa Lewis's club a few days later also seemed to think it was a bit too posh for me – I could tell from the look he gave me when he asked if I was sure I'd got the right place. The doors at the top of the steps leading up from Pall Mall must have been twenty foot high, deliberately designed to put the fear of God into peasants like me, sending us scurrying round to the servants' entrances and kitchens at the back. If the doors were high, the ceilings in the entrance lobby were even higher, more like a cathedral than any club I'd ever heard of. It was like I'd stepped through a time warp, or walked on to the set of a costume drama, complete with flunkeys in black tailcoats. Every man in sight was wearing a suit and tie and there weren't many women to be seen.

'Can I help you, madam?' one of the flunkeys enquired.

'I'm meant to be meeting Robert Lewis for lunch,' I said, horribly aware that my voice sounded too high and was echoing off the dark marble walls.

'Ah yes,' he purred, 'the General is waiting for you in the drawing room. If you would care to follow me.'

The General? Fuck! No one had ever mentioned that.

My heels were making a silly little clacking noise as I tried to keep up with him. Even the tilt of his shoulders looked disdainful, but maybe I was just being paranoid. To my relief, the sound changed as we passed through glass doors and on to wooden floors and finally fell blissfully silent as we stepped on to the thick carpets of the drawing room. Bookcases full of leather tomes stretched up to the vaulted ceilings above, and giant busts of dead statesmen stood on highly polished tables among well-tended piles of newspapers and magazines.

Grandpa looked very different as he rose from the chair he had been waiting in. His suit was immaculately pressed and his tie tightly knotted, nothing like the sloppy jumpers and baggy cords he wore when he was at home. He looked every inch the soldier, from his highly polished shoes to his gold cufflinks and neatly brushed hair.

'My dear,' he said, as he stepped forward, his hand outstretched for mine, leaning forward to peck me on the cheek, leaving the faintest whiff of cologne in his wake. 'It is so nice to see you again.'

'Really?' That didn't sound like quite the right response, but I was still genuinely surprised to have received his summons.

'Shall we have a sherry before we go through to the dining room?'

He gestured for me to sit beside him and nodded to the flunkey, who slid away to fetch the drinks. I'd never had sherry before but I didn't quite have the nerve to ask for a Diet Coke under the circumstances.

'I'm afraid the food here leaves a little to be desired,' he said, leaning close so no one else would hear. 'Some of us have been lobbying for a change in the menu but I'm afraid we are going to have to wait for a few more people to die before we start getting our way. I don't suppose you ever saw me as a moderniser.'

He gave a bark of laughter at his own joke and I smiled politely, not having a clue what he was on about.

'I was interested to read about your mother turning up like

219

that,' he said once the sherry had arrived. 'Must have been a bit of a shock.'

'Yeah.' That really was the best response I could manage.

'I've got a feeling I met her once. If you see her again, ask her if she ever worked at the Stork Club. Sure I remember a Maggie there.' I should imagine my mouth was hanging open at this stage of the conversation. 'How's the sherry?'

'Fine,' I said, taking a quick gulp, grateful for the warm glow it left in my chest as it passed through.

On the way to the dining room he paused in a room filled with old portraits, some of them bigger than life size. 'Bit of a family gallery, this,' he said, looking up at a picture of a man in black. 'That was my mother's father. One of Queen Victoria's Home Secretaries. A lot of people thought he would make it to Prime Minister, but he died. The pox, probably.' Another bark of a laugh. 'That one, there, the Bishop, he's a great-great-uncle of Luke's; wrote a book that was considered the last word on how the world was created, then along came Darwin and blew his whole theory out of the water. And that chap built many of the railways that allowed the British to take over India and the rest of the empire. These chaps, for better or worse, were the celebrities of their day. The equivalent to youngsters like you and Luke. Now they're just a load of gloomy old portraits. Hopefully you chaps will leave the world with something a bit more cheerful to look at.'

'I'm not sure *The Towers* is exactly cheerful,' I ventured, the glow of the sherry spreading pleasantly through me, settling my nerves.

'A few nice songs would be a good legacy to leave,' he said, before striding on towards the dining room.

'Seen young Luke recently?' he enquired, once we were seated in the dining room and he had ordered for both of us, writing our choices down on a pad left on the table and handing them to the waiter.

'No, not recently.'

'What about this chap you're being seen around town with?'

'Gerry?'

'Is he?'

'No, I mean that's his name.'

'Ah.' Another bark and this time I was laughing too. 'So, is it serious?'

'I don't think so.'

'Good.'

'Good?'

'Well, I don't think the girl Luke's hanging around with at the moment is the one for him either. Personally I think you're the one for him, but the rest of the family tell me I have to mind my own business and let him make up his own mind.'

A few sips of red wine had now joined the sherry and I felt extraordinarily happy. 'What's she like, this model?'

'Don't you know her, then? I assumed all you celebrities knew each other.'

'No, we don't,' I laughed. 'Our clubs aren't run quite like yours.'

'No, I suppose not. It was a smaller world in my day, a lot easier to find your way around, I dare say.' He paused to take

221

a slurp of soup, dabbing his chin carefully with the thick white linen serviette before going on. 'She's a pretty enough little thing, but if you ask my opinion – and I appreciate that you haven't – the boy's as much in love with you as you are with him. Just my humble opinion, of course.'

I concentrated hard on the soup, not sure what he expected me to say. No matter how much I spooned into my mouth, the bowl didn't seem to get any emptier. My head was whirling, all the emotions I'd been trying to keep a lid on rushing back to the surface.

'He was a bit hacked off that the record company wanted to record me without him,' I said eventually.

'I know, he told me. A bit old-fashioned of him, don't you think, in these days of equal women's rights?' He smiled mischievously. 'What you have to understand about Luke is that he's a bit on the competitive side. His brothers have been rather conspicuously successful, made pots of money in the City or whatever. He really wants to impress them all.'

'But he's successful too,' I protested. 'He was in one of the biggest-selling groups ever. And we reached the Christmas number-one spot.'

'I know all that, but I have more time than the rest of the family to keep up with these things. It's not a world they know much about and I'm afraid they have rather an old-fashioned attitude to the whole thing, so they don't always give him the credit he's due.'

'Snobbish, you mean,' I said, blushing at my own forwardness.

'Yes, I think you could say that. Pompous, even!'

We both barked together and one or two heads turned

222

very slightly in our direction. They probably thought I was his latest young mistress, which was fine by me. I no longer cared much what anyone thought. By the time we had reached the brandy (for him) and port (for me) we were both laughing pretty much constantly.

★ ★ ★ ★

'Did you ever work at a place called the Stork Club?' I asked Maggie next time I saw her, having invited her down to Docklands for supper.

'The Stork Club?' She sounded surprised. 'There's a name from the past. Why do you ask?'

'A friend of mine said he thought he knew you from there.'

'You have a friend who knew the Stork Club?'

'Robert Lewis,' I said.

'The General?' She laughed with what sounded like genuine affection. 'You know the General?'

'He's Luke's grandfather.'

'Is he? My God, what a small world. He was a character. Everyone knew the General. My God, he knew how to spend money. I think the family had to get the lawyers out to cut him off before he ruined them all. What a character.'

'Did you sleep with him?'

'Mind your own business, young lady.'

We both laughed at the primness of her answer, but she still chose not to say any more. For the rest of the evening she seemed to be a little bit lost in thought; lots of memories, I guess.

Chapter Twenty-One

I swear to God, I did not see it coming. When he turned up with his hair all brushed, his chin all shaved and a clean shirt, I thought nothing of it. When he told me he'd booked a table at a restaurant, I didn't smell a rat, even though he'd never done anything like that in all the time I'd known him. I didn't think anything when he fished the box out of his pocket and when he got off his chair and went down on one knee I just assumed he was doing up his shoelace, because he was wearing his desert boots as usual.

'What the fuck?' was my eloquent response to the question because I truly hadn't got a single part of me prepared. It was worse than winning a Bafta without having a speech ready. My mind went a complete blank. All I could think was that all the women at the surrounding tables had soppy looks on their faces, while all the men seemed to be averting their eyes from the embarrassing spectacle of one of their own making a prick of himself.

'Will you marry me?' Gerry asked again, opening the box and revealing a pretty ring.

'Jesus Christ, Gerry!'

Not the most romantic of responses, I know, but he had totally knocked the breath out of me.

'Well, will you?'

I could see that someone a few tables away was surreptitiously filming the scene on their phone, so it would probably be all over the Internet by the time we got home.

'I dunno, maybe. Too soon to tell. Jesus, Gerry, will you get back on the fucking chair,' I hissed.

'That's not exactly the reaction I was expecting,' he grumbled, sitting back down to his food.

'You've taken me by surprise a bit, mate.'

'Isn't that what's supposed to happen with marriage proposals?'

'My God, I don't know, I've never had one before. I don't think I can eat now. Why would you do it in a public place like that? It'll be all over the fucking papers tomorrow.'

'You'd better say yes, then.'

'No, Gerry!' Now I was shouting, which was really embarrassing, but I felt completely panic-stricken. I was having enough trouble holding on to my sanity as it was, I couldn't be thinking about marriage. Gerry was my best friend, I didn't want to lose that, but I didn't know if I wanted to marry him. I mean, nice guy and all that; good looking, kind, generous, patient. Oh God!

'I've got to go home,' I said, standing up and hurrying to the door.

'OK.' He looked all crestfallen, worried he'd done something wrong, which obviously he hadn't. He tossed a load of money on to the table as we fled from the restaurant to find our waiting driver and I swear a couple of flashes went off but I didn't bother to turn round.

He was taking my reaction so well, I felt like a real bitch. He held my hand tightly while I tried to pull my head together and started apologising over and over again. My head had been spinning ever since my lunch with Luke's grandpa. I had come away from the club walking on air, but as the days had passed I'd realised that nothing had actually changed. Just because Grandpa thought Luke and I were well suited didn't mean it was going to happen. It certainly wasn't enough of a reason for me to contact him, especially if he was going out with someone else. That would have been a really bitchy thing to do, keeping him dangling and risking upsetting his new relationship. But what if he was thinking the same thing, not contacting me because he had read about me and Gerry looking at houses in the sodding country?

'You don't have to apologise,' he said, kissing me gently on the cheek. 'And you don't have to give an answer yet. You never have to answer at all if you don't want to. Just think about it, OK?'

'You are so sweet.'

Now I felt like even more of a shit. No rushing around letting off guns for Gerry, and no stamping off in a huff and immediately going out with some bulimic little piece of modelling shit. (Sorry, getting carried away there.)

'Hang on to the ring too,' he said, pressing it into my hand. 'I might lose it.'

He came back to the penthouse with me and we finished

off a bottle of wine between us, just sitting staring at the view, not talking much, like an old married couple really. I found a slim silver chain for the ring and put it round my neck. He was as good as his word and didn't mention it again, didn't use it to make me feel guilty, just acted like the perfect gentleman, which made me feel like even more of a bitch for not being able to give him an answer. But marriage! I mean, shit! All I could see was me in one of those bloody integral laundry utility whatever rooms in the suburbs, trying to get dogs' hairs off my designer jeans.

'Do you know what I think?' he said a week or so later. 'I think you should have a go at mending some bridges with your dad.'

'I've tried. I rang and he just hung up on me.'

'Well, maybe we need to try again. Go round and see him.'

'You don't know what he's like. Once he's made his mind up about something nothing will change it.'

'It's worth a try though, isn't it?'

'I'm quite scared of him, to be honest. He can be fucking nasty when he's had a few.'

Gerry was being so reasonable and kind hearted; I was starting to feel like I was the one being unreasonable. Was I? Perhaps I was.

'But now you know how much he wanted you when you were a baby, that he wasn't going to let Maggie get rid of you, or put you up for adoption. Doesn't that change things a bit?'

'I know, I know.'

There was never a day when I didn't think how great it would be to be able to go back home, to just sit around the flat with the others, like we were still a normal family. It was the fear of how Dad would react if he found me there that stopped me from doing anything about it. But Gerry was right: I was an adult now, I should be the one making the decision to keep in contact.

'Why don't we go together?' he suggested.

'Would you do that for me?' I was touched.

'Of course I would. I'd like to meet him anyway. I liked your mum.'

'He's a bit different to her.'

My arguments were sounding more and more feeble and eventually they petered out altogether. I tried to pretend to Gerry that I had no worries about us just turning up on Dad's doorstep out of the blue, but actually I was bricking it as we drove down to the estate. I was expecting Gerry to be fazed by the sight of the gangs of kids hanging around in the shadows with their hoods up; we even passed an abandoned sofa that was smoking gently by the side of the road. But I guess when you've filmed in the slums of South America and Africa, and in war zones in the Middle East, a south-London estate doesn't seem so scary. Whatever the reason, his easy confidence was rubbing off on me a bit. Maybe spending the rest of my life with this guy wouldn't be such a terrible thing. I mean, I was sure he wouldn't make me live anywhere I didn't want to live, or do anything I didn't want to do.

I led the way up to our landing and held his hand tightly as I knocked on the door. I could hear shouting and swearing inside as they argued about who was going to answer it and then Mum's anxious face appeared behind the chain. The sight of me brought a flicker of a smile, swiftly followed by a frown of anxiety.

'Your dad's here,' she hissed.

'That's OK, Mum,' I said, annoyed that my voice was cracking with emotion. 'We've come to see all of you.'

She glanced behind me and saw Gerry, giving him a nod of recognition, but still looking worried.

'Who is it?' Dad shouted from the kitchen.

'Tell him,' I said, when she hesitated.

'It's Steffi.'

There was silence behind her as everyone in the flat waited to see what would happen next. After a few moments his face appeared above hers.

'What do you want?' he demanded.

'Hi, Dad,' I said, trying to sound like this was a normal family visit. 'We thought we'd pop in.'

'Hi, Mr McBride.' Gerry stepped forward, putting his hand through the gap in the door, risking having it slammed on him. 'I'm Gerry, it's really good to meet you at last.'

Dad ignored the hand and Gerry retracted it without showing any sign of discomfort.

'What do you want?' Dad repeated.

Mum seemed to lose her patience. 'Oh my Lord. Can we have this conversation inside without all the neighbours staring?'

She flicked the chain off and opened the door so quickly Dad didn't have a chance to protest. Gerry steered me in before anyone changed their minds. It felt strange to suddenly be enveloped in all the familiar smells of Mum's cooking and the various aftershaves and perfumes my brothers and sisters wore, mingling with cigarette smoke.

'Hi.' Gerry tried again with the handshake. 'I'm Gerry.'

This time Dad gave in and shook his hand. Other faces were appearing at the doors along the corridor as everyone's courage seemed to build.

'Hey, Steff.' Jeremiah was the first to speak up, then the others found their courage too.

Mum led us into the sitting room, with everyone else crowding in behind us. It all looked just as I remembered, but I'd forgotten the overwhelming feeling of claustrophobia, so many bodies in such a small space, so many personalities vying for dominance.

Gerry looked entirely comfortable, settling into a chair, introducing himself to the rest of them. It was as if Dad was being upstaged as the alpha male of the pack and I wasn't sure how he was going to take that. He was standing quietly in the background, but I felt he was brewing up like a volcano.

'I was just making a meal,' Mum said. 'You will both stay, won't you?'

'That would be great,' Gerry jumped in before I could answer. 'Steff has told me so much about your cooking.'

'Oh, it's nothing.' Mum almost wriggled with pleasure. I hoped Gerry wasn't laying it on too thick.

'Would there be time for Mr McBride and me to go for a drink and get acquainted before tea?'

I couldn't believe it. How was Gerry finding the nerve for this?

'We've got time,' Dad replied. 'Come on, then.'

'Your dad likes him,' Mum said as the door slammed behind them, sounding as surprised as I was.

By the time they came back, Dad was nicely balanced on the edge of being too drunk – just at that point where he was at his most amiable. One more and there was a risk he would tip over into anger and violence. Maybe he'd just had a few beers and no spirits. Gerry was pretending he was at the same point, but I knew he wasn't. The chances were he'd managed to only have one drink to Dad's three or four. If the others had been planning to go out, they had all changed their plans now, all wanting to be there for the meal to get to know the wonderful Gerry. I can't deny it was an incredible relief, but I was also a bit pissed off that they were all so keen to hear about his adventures behind the camera and seemed totally disinterested in everything that had happened to me since I was last home. I mean, did a Bafta mean nothing to these people? (Only kidding. Well, mostly.) I couldn't believe it; we were all sitting round the table like we were the fucking Waltons.

'So, Gerry,' Dad said, as if the two of them were the oldest mates in the world, 'when are you going to be making an honest woman of our Steffi?'

That silenced the room at a stroke as everyone turned to stare at him. Gerry didn't look remotely bothered.

'I'd do it tomorrow if I could persuade her.' He grinned in a way that they no doubt thought was 'boyishly charming' but I thought was a bit slimy.

It suddenly dawned on me why he had insisted on coming to meet the family: he was recruiting them to his fucking cause.

My best friend, the shoulder I always used to cry on, was consorting with the fucking enemy. 'Pull yourself together, Steff,' I told myself, 'they are not the enemy, they are your family and Gerry is doing a great job at reuniting you with them.'

'You marry this man, Steffi,' Dad boomed, like some jovial shopping-mall Santa. 'Or I'm going to want to know the reason why not.'

It probably would have sounded like pub banter to anyone who hadn't lived with him for twenty-odd years, but I knew it was a direct order, and so did all the others. Mum, bless her, immediately started bustling around giving everyone second helpings and everyone else found something fascinating to stare at on their plates.

I hauled as much oxygen in as I could manage, trying to quell the rising panic in my chest. I couldn't find any words to make light of the situation. It actually felt as if someone had tied my tongue up. Mum did her best to cover up the tension, but it didn't work. After that things went from bad to worse as I suggested we should leave because I had to be up early in the morning and Dad insisted on taking Gerry back down to the pub for a few more drinks. As the hours ticked by I began to feel angry as well as fearful of what state Dad would be in by the time they finally rolled back. If Gerry was too drunk to drive we would have to spend the night on the couch and the whole horror would stretch out to the morning. I was desperately craving the peace and solitude of the penthouse. The angrier I became, the more I realised I didn't have to put up with it if I didn't want to. I was an adult. I could make my own decisions about what I wanted to do. I phoned a taxi

company and gave them the address. An hour later I was back
in the penthouse, feeling horribly alone. I had so wanted to
be accepted back into the bosom of the family, but when I
was I'd felt like I was going to suffocate.

Chapter Twenty-Two

'They want to do a *Meet the Real Steffi McBride* programme,'
Dora announced. 'You know the sort of thing: you on
the stage, the audience packed with celebrities, planted
questions and you singing some songs. Prime-time Saturday-
night spot.'

'I thought they just did that sort of thing with really big
stars,' I said, puzzled.

'You're about as big as they get at the moment, darling,'
she drawled.

I wished I hadn't said that, because now it sounded like I
was fishing for compliments and I didn't know how to react.

'Do you think I should do it?' I asked eventually.

'Might be fun. They would let you sing whatever you
wanted, and they would pay a lot.'

'OK, whatever you think.'

'Are you all right, darling? Having man trouble?' Dora had
an uncanny knack of reading my moods just from the tone of
my voice.

'Yeah, a bit.'

The visit home had left me so confused. It was really nice
that Gerry wanted me to marry him so much, even if it was

a bit of an underhand way of going about it. It was also nice that I was back in touch with Dad, sort of. But it was so much pressure. Gerry had been totally taken aback when I laid into him about the whole thing when I saw him the next day.

'I thought you would be happy to be reunited with your dad,' he protested.

'I am, but you could at least have discussed what you were planning with me. It would have been nice to have been a bit prepared.'

'There was no plan,' he said. 'I was just going with the flow. You really have got to stop thinking the worst of everyone. I just love you, that's all.'

So then I felt like a complete dog turd on his shoe, but I still couldn't raise my spirits enough to even act graciously. The moodier I became, the more reasonable, open and sunny he was. There just didn't seem to be a single fault with the bloody man.

Dad had rung me several times since that evening, usually after he'd got back from the pub, telling me what a great chap Gerry was and saying he wanted to put the past behind him, make a new start. Having been desperate to be back in touch with him, I now dreaded the long, rambling phone calls. Drink now seemed to make him fucking miserable and sorry for himself, but at least that was an improvement on violent. He kept talking about 'getting things off his chest once and for all', but when I asked him what he was talking about he would go all mysterious and evasive and I couldn't be bothered to ask any more.

I'm sure they all meant well. I'm sure Dad genuinely liked

236

Gerry and thought he would be a good husband; and of course he was right. Gerry was an incredibly nice guy and he would always treat me well. But at the same time …

I didn't stop seeing Gerry, but I often told him I was busy in the evenings without telling him who I was busy with. Sometimes it was celebrity functions, which the publicity people liked me to turn up to in order to keep Nikki in the magazines. I had perfected a technique for those sorts of dos. If I accepted an invitation to an opening of a club or a film premiere, I would get the girls at the studio to make me up after work, borrow a frock from Wardrobe, take the limo to the red carpet, have my picture taken for the magazines, go inside and walk straight out the back, where the limo would be waiting to take me home. Sometimes I would take one of the younger blokes from *The Towers*, just to keep the reporters guessing, but the boys always wanted to hang around in the hope that they would pull some dozy Page Three girl. I think I might have hoped that it would piss Gerry off as well if I was photographed with other men, but he never seemed bothered. He hated those sorts of media events as much as I did and he obviously wasn't fooled for a second into thinking that I was having a fling with anyone else from the cast. Sometimes his self-confidence and philosophical outlook on life could be quite annoying; occasionally I would just have liked him to get unreasonably pissed off with me when I behaved badly, rather than being all understanding and indulging me the whole time. It's no wonder the poor sodding men say they don't understand what it is that women want from them when we don't know ourselves, is it?

Quentin James had taken to ringing me quite often, as if we were old friends or something and, spookily, it was almost beginning to feel like we were. So when he rang, saying, 'Maggie and I are having dinner this evening, want to join us?' it seemed quite natural to say yes. He'd booked a table at a restaurant in the Berkeley Hotel, just along from Harvey Nichols (scary how quickly I'd got used to going to places like this) and they were both already there when I arrived.

'My God, you look gorgeous,' I said to Maggie, kissing her on both cheeks in true showbiz fashion before pecking at Quentin and sitting down. In fact, she actually did look gorgeous, unrecognisable as the woman I first saw across Quentin's office. Whatever the surgeons had done to her had given her a sort of Lauren Bacall meets Charlotte Rampling look now that everything had settled down, kind of bony and haughty. She didn't look at all out of place among the sleek Knightsbridge and Belgravia ladies on the surrounding tables.

'Thank you, darling,' she purred. 'It has been agony but it is finally worth it.'

We ordered food, but not much as we were both keen to lose a few pounds. Quentin had no such inhibitions and tucked into a full three courses, making me feel bloody hungry as I nibbled on a Caesar salad.

'I've been asked to do a television "audience-with" thing,' I explained, 'and I really want to get into a mini skirt and not look like an elephant.'

'I heard about that,' Quentin muttered through a mouthful of foie gras. 'Half my clients have been asked to be in the audience.'

'How is your singing going?' I asked Maggie.

'Brilliant. I've been signed to do an album of country covers. Dolly Parton, Tammy Wynette, all the standard weepies, giving them a bit of a clubby, jazzy edge.'

'It's a new slant on fusion,' Quentin added, like he knew something about music, which I was pretty sure he didn't. He struck me as a basic *Abba's Greatest Hits* man, but I didn't bother to say.

'She's being modest,' Quentin went on and Maggie smiled, modestly. 'She's touring all over the country and every venue has sold out, almost overnight.'

'Well done,' I said. I genuinely did feel pleased. I could imagine just how much it would mean to her.

'Thanks,' she said. 'It's all a bit overwhelming, and I've been working on my book at the same time as all this has been going on.'

'Your book?' This was one surprise after another and I was beginning to feel a bit punch drunk.

'My autobiography. Quentin set up this incredible deal, but they want delivery like yesterday, while I'm still fresh in everyone's minds from the programme and the media coverage.'

'Autobiography?' I realised I was beginning to sound like some sort of monosyllabic dumbo, but I was having real trouble getting my head round all this new information.

'Well, it's not completely "auto", if you know what I mean,' she laughed. 'Quentin found me this brilliant ghost to work with.'

'Will Dad and everything be in it?' I asked, feeling a growing sense of doom, like people must have felt in the old days when they all believed the atomic bomb was going to be dropped at any moment.

'God, yes, we wouldn't have got such a good serialisation deal from the papers without promising to talk about all that.'

What could I say? I felt like I was about to be raped but I knew it was all my own fault. I'd started this whole thing with my fancy ideas about becoming an actress and I was being swept away in the avalanche; even my conception was going to become public property now. This would finish my relationship with Dad once and for all.

'Dad can be quite a private person,' I said, choosing my words carefully. 'This could send him mental.'

'I think your father is starting to see the advantages of co-operating with the media,' Quentin said.

'Dad is?' Yet again he'd managed to shock me. 'You've talked to him?'

'We wanted to check a few things.' Quentin was being deliberately vague. 'We've been talking about other possibilities.'

'I'd really like to read this book of yours,' I said, suddenly unable to manage any more of my salad and emptying my wine glass instead.

'Of course.' Maggie put her hand over mine and squeezed reassuringly. 'I'll ask the ghost to email stuff through to you as he writes it, shall I?'

'Great.' I coughed, extracting my hand from under hers to cover my mouth. I was fighting an overwhelming urge to be alone, to escape from all of them. Dad had been talking to Quentin? About what?

'I hear you've got a cameo in boyfriend Pete's documentary,' Quentin said as he paused between courses.

'Oh my God, that was so embarrassing,' I said, suddenly remembering the whole scene, still able to feel the impact of my boot on the cameraman's shin. 'How did you know about that? It isn't on the Internet, is it?'

'He's my client, remember?'

How could I have forgotten? This was like a surreal dream. This man had tentacles everywhere, even into a squat on my old estate.

'How the fuck did that happen anyway?' I wanted to know. 'How did you get to meet him?'

'I asked your old girlfriends for an introduction. I wanted to hear his music, see if I could introduce him to a few people. He was one of the highest-profile news stories in the country for a few days, remember? He was hot and everyone wanted a piece of him.'

'The police were looking for him, weren't they?'

It seemed to sum up everything about Quentin. The whole London police force hadn't been able to find Pete, but he had managed it. Maybe he actually was the devil.

'Oh, that got sorted out,' he said airily. 'I introduced him to a lawyer who knows how to make those sorts of charges disappear. Since you weren't lodging any sort of complaint they didn't want to bother with unnecessary paperwork, especially if he was going to be a celebrity.'

'So you got him a music deal?' I was still trying to imagine Pete and Quentin even being in the same room together.

'The man has street cred; he's known to deal drugs and

carry guns, that's exactly the sort of market the record companies want to reach. He also has the cachet of being one of your exes.'

One of my exes? My God, that made me sound like Kate Moss or someone.

'Has he even written a single song since leaving school?' I asked.

'The record company's working on that. They've teamed him up with some people. And his dad's helping.' Quentin shrugged. 'The money is mainly going to be in live gigs and deejaying, that sort of thing.'

'If he turns up,' I said, remembering Pete's general reluctance to get out of bed most days.

'His mother's working on that side of things. She seems a pretty tough character.'

I had to hand it to him. Quentin might be a bit of a prize wanker, but he certainly knew his business and didn't mind getting his hands dirty.

'I got a letter from your old friend the other day,' Maggie said brightly.

'What old friend?' I had no idea what she was talking about.

'Robert Lewis. He said he'd had lunch with you and that had set him to reminiscing about the old days.'

'Does he want to renew the acquaintance?'

'Invited me to lunch.'

'His posh club?'

'No, Rules. We went there a few times in the old days, a bit of a walk down memory lane. We had dinner there with John Betjeman once.'

'Who's he?'

The two of them exchanged a look that really pissed me off – that 'my God, the young people of today know nothing' look – but I let it pass. I dare say there are a few people under the age of a hundred I know about that they are unaware of too.

'Famous poet,' Maggie said. 'He was a friend of Robert's family, I think.'

I made a mental note of the name, as usual. I would look him up when I got home and try one of his books. I'd always fancied having a go at reading poetry. Dave had always said I'd like it, but somehow I'd never quite got my head round it. It would make it more relevant if it had something to do with Luke's family.

'So, have you planned the songs you're going to do in this show?' Quentin asked.

'I've got a few ideas,' I said vaguely, nervous about telling him anything in case it ended up on the front pages of the papers in the morning. 'And the production company's got a few ideas.'

'You should do a duet with Maggie,' Quentin suggested, like the idea had only just occurred to him. 'The viewers would love that: mother and daughter reunited in song.'

'They've already seen us reunited in plastic surgery,' I muttered.

'The public can never get too much of a good thing,' he grinned. 'If you can make 'em cry, they will always be back for more.'

'Don't be embarrassing, Q,' Maggie protested, a bit half-heartedly I thought. 'It's her show, she can choose whoever she wants.'

'You could have Pete on as well, doing his debut single,' he went on, as if she hadn't spoken. 'That would get the kids watching.'

'Why don't we just have all your clients on the stage at once,' I suggested, 'like a giant gospel choir of sleazebags. No offence, Maggie.'

'Really?' She arched a freshly plucked eyebrow.

'I didn't mean you, I meant all the others.'

She shrugged, apparently accepting the inevitable, and I felt guilty.

'Well,' I backtracked, 'maybe it's not such a dumb idea – the duet, I mean.'

Quentin didn't miss a beat or a mouthful. 'I'll ring the production company and have a word.'

My schedule at *The Towers* had become more and more demanding as the producers tried to milk Nikki for all she was worth, so I didn't get the time to have as much input into *Meet the Real Steffi McBride* as I would have liked. Dora was struggling to get me a bit of script approval in my contract on *The Towers*, but the producers were holding out against it, even though they had been happy to consult me unofficially. I suppose they thought if they gave in to one of us they would have to give in to others and the whole thing would become unmanageable. Some of the recent storylines hadn't been that brilliant, to be honest, and seemed more like excuses for Nikki to get her kit off for the cameras. I was still getting away with making her credible, just, but it was becoming increasingly hard. The idea of doing a stage show, where I could perfect the performance and then repeat it night after night, was becoming increasingly attractive.

Chapter Twenty-Three

Maggie's ghostwriter was obediently emailing material through to me every few days and I would print it off and take it into work with me to read. I have to say, it was a gripping story. It sounded like she had come from pretty much the same sort of family as Gerry – really straight and maybe a bit boring. Rebelling at 15, she left home in search of adventure in London, and found plenty of that. She became a Page Three model within a few days of arriving in the city (lying about her age) and was working for an escort agency within a few months. She wanted to act and sing, but everywhere she turned she was told she needed an 'equity card', which was like a union membership, but she couldn't get one unless she was in work – bit of a Catch-22, really. One sort of work that would get her the card was stripping, so that was how she ended up at Raymond's Revue Bar.

Bloody hell. That was a bit of a thought-provoker. Would I have been willing to put myself through all that in order to get into the business? Yeah, I guess I would have done. And would I have ended up in the same horrible mess? Almost certainly. The further I read into the story, the more I could identify with her. She painted a scary picture of what life in

London must have been like in the 1970s and all in all it made me grateful that I'd been born when I had.

As the days passed and the pages kept arriving I came to terms with the idea of Maggie spilling the beans. Even when she reached the part describing her fling with Dad, which only took a few pages if I'm honest, I didn't think it was going to be too hurtful to Mum. When it came to talking about giving me away it was a bit hard to read and it took several tries before I was able to do it without choking up, but she did have the grace to make Mum out as a sort of modern-day saint.

Lulled into a false sense of relief, I wasn't braced for the next blow, which came from a completely different direction and knocked the breath out of me all over again. I should have realised that Quentin was up to something the night we had dinner together, but it honestly hadn't occurred to me that Dad might also be writing a book until the serialisation came out in the *Daily Mirror*. The whole concept of Dad, the man who thought reading anything other than the *Daily Mirror* or *News of the World* was 'a bit poofy', writing a book was almost too surreal to take in.

'My dad is your fucking client too?' I raged down the phone on the morning the serialisation appeared. 'Have you signed up my entire fucking family?'

'Not quite,' he chuckled, 'you're still holding out, but I'm hopeful you'll see the light soon.'

'Couldn't you have at least warned me this was coming?'

'Would have felt obliged to if you were my client,' he said, smarmy git. 'But as it is I had to protect my existing clients' confidentiality.'

'That is such crap, Quentin, and you know it.' I hung up, angry but pretty impressed at the same time.

Dad's story was very different to Maggie's. The first extract in the paper mainly covered his childhood, up till the time he came across to England from Ireland in search of work on his 18th birthday. The main thrust of the story was his relationship with his father. I'd never met my grandfather, never even heard Dad talk about him, and now I knew why. The man was a monster. He beat the children to within an inch of their lives, as well as his wife, and had sex with all of them as if it was his divine right. How the ghostwriter had got Dad to open up about such personal stuff, when he had kept it all bottled up for so long, God alone knows, but he had made up for lost time. Every gory detail was there, but at the same time he painted kind of a nice picture of growing up in Ireland in the 1960s, buried away deep in the countryside. There was obviously terrible poverty in the family as well as the cruelty, but Dad had managed to describe a way of life that I would imagine not many people still experience, at least not in Britain. As I read his words I felt so sorry for the small boy telling the story, and for the first time ever I actually understood why Dad was the way he was; why he drank to try to silence the voices in his memory and why he had been guarding the family's privacy so fiercely. I felt sad and guilty that my success had forced him to reveal so many of his secrets, but at the same time I felt a sort of relief that it was now all out in the open. Maybe he would be happier and more at peace now, not having to carry all this around in his head.

Gerry came round that evening, having read the pieces himself and knowing just how badly rocked I was feeling. He didn't try to talk about it; he was just there for me, his arm around me, comforting me.

'Your dad's an OK guy,' he'd said soon after our disastrous visit home, making me even angrier with him. 'He's had a hard time.'

Now I realised how right Gerry had been and how intuitive and how understanding. Maybe it was a bloke thing; maybe they all have some silent language when they're drinking together that lets them instinctively know about one another's wounds, whereas we girls would have to vocalise the whole thing to get it out there.

'Are you coming to the recording of this *Meet the Real …* thing?' I asked later in the evening as we cuddled on the sofa watching the pleasure boats covered in fairy lights gliding past on the river.

'Nah,' he laughed. 'That's just for celebrities.'

'What do you mean?'

'They're not letting any civilians in.'

'I could get you in,' I protested. 'I'll have a word.'

'No, really, I know my place.'

'That is such bullshit.'

'Listen, I spend my whole time waiting around in television studios for things to happen; it won't break my heart to have a night off.'

To be honest, I was a bit sad that he didn't want to be there to see me in my hour of triumph, but I could hardly admit that, could I? Not when he was being so modest and matter-of-fact about the whole thing. It would have made me sound like a right prima donna, so I just left it.

I rang Dad later that evening, once I'd collected my thoughts a bit.

'Read your story in the paper, Dad.'

'Yeah?' his voice was slow and slurred. 'Well, you don't want to be believing everything you read in those rags.'

'Are you saying it's not true?'

'I'm saying nothing.' He sounded belligerent and I didn't feel like fighting.

'OK. I love you, Dad.'

'Hah!'

I have no idea what he meant by that because he hung up and when I tried to ring back no one was answering the phones again. I could imagine that seeing his words edited up by a paper must have been a bit of a shock, but then he had been the one to say that reporters were all 'slimy' anyway, so maybe he would have anticipated it. I knew the newspaper would have picked out all the shocking bits from the book and left out a lot of the parts that he probably thought gave a more accurate, rounded picture of his life. Welcome to my world, Dad.

The next day there was another extract, all about his meeting with Maggie. There were pictures too, showing a surprisingly handsome young man. I'm not sure I would have recognised him. He and Maggie would have made a good-looking couple. I could see why she might have been attracted to him that night in the club. He talked about Mum too, and it was obvious how much he loved her. I guess the ghostwriter must have helped him with those words because they weren't any I'd ever heard him utter, or could even imagine him saying. Dad prided himself on being a hard man and hard men didn't go in for all that romantic stuff, but the emotions rang true as they were written. It made me cry to think how much it would mean to Mum to read those words. Then he talked about my birth and how he was determined to bring me up and do his best to guide me in life. You can forgive someone a lot of sins when you know that they were willing to do something like that for you. I didn't bother to ring him that evening; I felt we both knew where we stood now.

Chapter Twenty-Four

The whole *Meet the Real …* concept was about as fake as it was possible to get. The producers went after every possible celebrity they could think of, anyone who was currently hot, plus some evergreens from the past. (I have to admit there were a few old ones I hadn't got a clue about, but I dare say they were famous to someone.)

There were singers and actors, footballers and footballers' wives, models and weather girls, comedians and politicians, presenters of every kind of television programme from newsreaders to DIY experts. Anyone who had a face that would be recognisable to any part of the viewing public was herded in. The weird thing was, it was actually starting to seem normal to me, being surrounded by strangers with familiar faces. Perhaps it was my brain's way of coping with the fact that all these famous people were gathering there for me. I mean, there was a strong danger that I would completely freeze on stage if I really thought about it. Best just to go through the whole thing in a sort of haze, like I was just leafing through the latest edition of *OK!*.

'Celebrity World' might be fake, but it's a wonderfully comfortable place to be. It's clean, safe and friendly, somewhere where we all know our places, a sort of Disney World where the characters are actually real people. Celebrities generally are kind and polite to each other when they meet. They bitch a bit, and stage the odd fight for the benefit of the press, but it's not like the real world — at least, not like the real world that I came from. In the world I started out in people beat each other up and shouted abuse at one another — in Celebrity World, that generally only happens when the dialogue has been written for us by scriptwriters, or publicists like Quentin.

The grind of our daily existence is eased by make-up women and hairdressers and drivers and gofers. If we want to we can eat out for every meal and we don't have to worry about how to heat the house next winter or whether our kids are going to be murdered by their schoolmates. None of us can live in Celebrity World all the time, of course, and we still have to step back through the looking glass to deal with things like divorce and cancer, road accidents and broken hearts, but as long as we're in the studios and at the clubs and parties we can pretend the real world doesn't exist, that everything in our false world is shiny and happy, at least for the short time that we inhabit it. We are living among the gods. Oh my Lord, I've gone all Greek Myth now …

A select few of this sparkly audience were given written questions to ask me, questions that would trigger off pre-prepared anecdotes and jokes that the director had rehearsed with me. To start with I was a bit uncomfortable and then it all started to seem rather camp and fun, like a Liza Minnelli or Judy Garland concert: pure showbiz glitz and smarm for all to see through. Every person in that room knew the score, knew what was expected of them, knew that the exposure would benefit them too, even if it was only a few seconds on screen as the cameras panned around the audience looking for them.

Towards the end of the show, someone was briefed to ask a question about Maggie and I was going to say something glib, she would then come on to tumultuous applause and we would sing together. Someone else would ask about Pete and I would make a joke about being shot in the street (always a good laugh to be had from that sort of material – not!) and then Pete would come on and look hard while performing his newly released single.

When they told me Mum and Dad and the rest of the family were going to be in the audience as well, I didn't believe them at first. Well, I believed that they had been asked, but I didn't believe Dad would actually show up. Still, even after all this time, I was underestimating the persuasive powers of Quentin James (Dad now had a product to promote just like the rest of us, of course). Not only were they all there, they were all newly attired in designer clothes (had that been part of the bribe?) and all smiling, apart from Dad who looked embarrassed – as he should have been for agreeing to betray his own principles so blatantly. The scriptwriters had even written a short piece of banter to go between me on the stage and him in the audience, something that would show we had been through hard times but still loved each other underneath, to show forgiveness on my part and contrition on his.

'This is a corny crock of shit,' I told Dora during a break in rehearsals.

'Sure it is,' she growled, 'but the higher your star can ascend now the more I can ask for you when you agree to do *Sweet Charity*.'

'I haven't agreed yet?' I asked, surprised.

'You're playing hard to get.'

'You'll let me know when I make up my mind, will you?'

'You bet.'

What I liked about Dora was her total refusal ever to rise to any bait I might dangle in front of her. We both knew the score, and we both knew that the other knew the score. We didn't have to pretend anything to each other; it was bloody restful.

'This,' I said, gesturing around the studio, 'is all starting to seem a bit like *This Is Your Life*, set to music.'

'That's about the shape of it.'

I could see Dora was really enjoying herself; she even managed to raise a smile when Pete spotted her and came over. He didn't trouble himself to remove his shades but he did grin broadly, reminding me of how charming he'd been when I first fell for him.

'Hey, it's the scary old lady. How's it going, scary old lady?'

'It's going just fine, Peter,' she replied, playing up to the schoolmarm role he was allotting her for the amusement of the gaggle of friends he had surrounding him.

'This is my band, man,' he told me when I gave them a bit of a look. I could remember most of them from school and this was the first I had ever heard of them being a band, but that was the producer's problem, not mine.

'Whatever, Pete.'

It was scheduled for Maggie and me to sing Gloria Gaynor's 'I Will Survive' number and 'The Best is Yet To Come', which Garland and Minnelli had once sung together. We were then to end the show together singing 'A Little Time', which I thought was a bit weird since it was supposed to be about a man cheating on a woman, saying he needed 'a bit of time' and 'some space' and all that. I voiced my doubts to the producer but he was adamant that it would work, that the audience would remember me singing it with Luke and that would give it an extra poignancy. It seemed to me he was teetering on the edge of really bad taste, but I could see he was under pressure and didn't need any sort of hissy fit from me at this late stage.

Ultimately you have to do what you're told in these situations and it didn't seem such a big deal. Celebrities may look like the most important people in any gathering, but actually we're just the puppets. It's the writers and the producers and directors, cameramen and executives who really have the power.

I had never felt stage fright like the feelings that gripped me as I prepared myself to step out on to the stage that evening. I knew it was all being recorded and I knew they could always stop and go back if I messed up or if anything went wrong technically, but it was still going to be me out on the stage with every pair of eyes on me. It was still going to be me that everyone was going to judge tonight. Would they be going away muttering about how I didn't have the talent to hold together a showcase like this? Or were they going to be whispering to one another that 'a star is born'?

There were so many people out there that I wanted to impress, wanted to make love me; not just the celebrities and the eventual television audience, but my own family as well. I was standing up in front of everyone as if I was someone special. I'd bloody well better be special, then, or I was going to look like a real dick. Most of all, I wanted Dad to see that everything was going to be OK; that the embarrassment of being in the public eye and having the reporters 'going through our bins' was going to be worth it if it brought us all together and meant we could be truthful with each other.

The moment I walked out on to the stage I felt every care and worry lifting from my shoulders. It was the most incredible feeling of power and comfort. I just knew I was going to be able to hold the audience's attention and make them enjoy themselves. Some of the scripted jokes were pretty lame, let's be honest, but there were ways of delivering them that could still be funny enough and would make everyone feel they were in safe hands.

The best thing was being able to see Mum and Dad in the front row. She was cuddling up to him, probably trying to calm his nerves as well since he was going to have to perform a bit. Our little banter came pretty early, which I should imagine was a big relief to him, and I was really surprised how well he did it. No one would have guessed if he was scared, he sounded authoritative and loving and funny. Maybe the old sod can actually act after all. I felt so proud of him when the audience laughed at his line and applauded and Mum was glowing up at him all lovingly. He was like a big kid being picked out for praise at school assembly. That's what it must have been like when they were young, before all the pressures came. The reason she had been willing to take me on as a daughter must have been because she loved him so much. That was why she had stayed with him over the years, putting up with the beatings and bullying, knowing that the young man she was in love with was still there underneath all the arrogance and bluster he used to disguise his fears.

Someone asked the slightly cheeky question about drugs and guns, which allowed me to make the matching cheeky response and to bring on Pete. I hadn't heard his group in rehearsals and I was quite impressed. It reminded me of happy times in the squat when he used to beat out a rhythm on anything and everything, and Pete looked really sexy doing it. If he could hold it together, he just might end up being a real star.

There was a bit more banter with me and the audience, all of us talking to one another like we were old friends. It hadn't been that long since I would have been one of the people watching the programme and really believing that the person on the stage truly was best mates with Victoria Beckham, Jordan, Simon Cowell and Ant and Dec. In fact, I'd only ever met any of them for about thirty seconds – but, hey, this was acting too, wasn't it?

Then on came Maggie and the audience went wild. I guess everyone who has made it in show business, or one of the allied professions, knows how easily their careers could all have gone wrong. They all know that with a few different breaks they could have been the ones ending up in an Earl's Court bedsit with a face like a bagful of old spanners. It was like they were acknowledging that Maggie had paid her dues to the business, proved herself in the school of hard knocks and still refused to give up. All those corny song lyrics come to mind. Not just 'I Will Survive', but 'I'm Still Standing', 'Je Ne Regrette Rien' (impressed?) and 'My Way'. Everyone loves a survivor and God knows Maggie was one of them.

We sang our first two songs together and received standing ovations both times, which would have been better if the audience hadn't been told to stand up by the floor managers, but still felt good.

The band struck up for 'A Little Time'. The director had put me at the front of the stage, with Maggie a few paces behind. I'd protested that we should be side by side, particularly as she had the first verse, but they told me it was my show and they didn't want it to look like Maggie was trying to upstage me. Everyone seemed to be happy about it, so I didn't argue.

I was actually watching Mum and Dad and the rest of the family as I waited for Maggie to start, feeling comfortable that the show was nearly in the bag, and really happy with the way everything had turned out.

The singing started behind me, but it wasn't Maggie. I swung round, taken by surprise, in time to see Maggie stepping back into the shadows and Luke coming out, singing the same words he'd sung to me so often while we were making the other show. I was completely shocked. I'd had no inkling that anyone was planning to spring this on me. The lyrics were all about him taking a break in our relationship, which was pretty much what the public thought had happened to us.

He looked so beautiful and I knew he was still the man of my dreams. We had done the song so often I could sing my part without any rehearsals, but I wasn't able to keep the emotional catch out of my voice, which must have made it all the more affecting for the audience. They must have been able to see how desperately in love with him I was, even if the song ends with me telling him that while he's been away I've learned that I actually don't need him, that I had had the time to find the courage to 'call it off'.

Everyone in that audience knew about Gerry; they'd read about us a thousand times in the magazines. They might have been able to see that I was in love with Luke, but they also knew I was empowered and in control of the relationship as well, that I could make a life without him if I had to, and all women love to see that. I knew, as we were singing, that he wouldn't have agreed to do the song and to take me by surprise in this way if he hadn't wanted us to get back together again. It was like I'd been given permission to relight my fantasies, to believe once again that my dream of being with Luke Lewis, the great love of my childhood, could become a reality.

By the time the song had come to an end, he had walked downstage to me and, taking me in his arms, he kissed me passionately for all to see. It wasn't one of those friendly, show-business stage kisses; it was the kiss of a lover.

'How did this happen?' I asked him as the applause thundered over us.

'Maggie and Grandpa made me come to my senses,' he grinned. 'They pointed out that there was no way I would ever be happy if I let you get away and suggested I should grow up a bit.'

I glanced across at Maggie who was standing in the wings, watching, and mouthed a thank-you. The audience kept applauding and cheering until eventually Maggie and Pete came on to join us as well and the band struck up with 'There's no business like show business', which Maggie and I had rehearsed just in case an extra number was needed. Pete looked a bit of a fish out of water, but still managed to keep his cool by beat boxing along to the rhythm. The floor managers were working the audience and everyone was joining in, like the finale of some surreal pantomime, which I suppose in a way it was. I could see that even Dad was singing along, which was something I'd never seen happen outside a pub before.

I walked off stage in a cloud of happiness. Luke had his arm around my shoulders and Mum and Dad were walking behind with Maggie as if they were all the oldest friends in the world, my brothers and sisters bouncing along behind, their mouths hanging open as they ricocheted off one celebrity after another. Drinks and snacks had been laid on in a green room behind the scenes. As we walked into the room I saw Gerry waiting to surprise me with a huge bouquet of flowers and all the joy was suddenly silenced. It was as if someone had hit the pause button on the iPod inside my head, the one providing the soundtrack to my euphoria.

I saw Gerry's eyes moving from me to Luke and then back down along his arm to the silver chain around my neck. Luke saw it too and pulled away but it was too late; I'd seen the hurt before Gerry was able to hide it again behind his jaunty, worldly air of cool. In that second I saw him realise the truth and despair.

'Gerry.' I forced a smile and went across to peck him on the cheek.

'These are for you,' he said, passing the flowers over. 'I've been watching on the monitors. You were fantastic.'

'Thank you,' I said. There was an awkward pause as we both tried to think what to say next.

'Listen,' I said. 'I'm sorry.'

'No need,' he said, 'not your fault.'

How could anyone be that understanding when they were having their heart broken in public? He had to be the strongest man I had ever met, and I was about to let him go.

I slipped the chain off from round my neck and pressed the ring into his hand. 'Thanks for asking. It was really sweet and I do love you. It's just …'

'Please,' he interrupted. 'You don't have to explain anything. I've got to dash, I just wanted to pop by and give you those and tell you how brilliant you are. See you at the studio tomorrow.'

'Yes.'

As I watched him go I felt like the meanest person on the face of the earth, but within a few seconds I had been engulfed in a crowd of people, all telling me that I was absolutely the greatest thing since sliced bread. Whatcha gonna do? You have to go with the flow, don't you? You have to keep the dream alive.

www.steffimcbride.com